Stepping from the Shadows

STEPPING FROM THE SHADOWS

Patricia A. McKillip, Patricia A

LC: 81-69151

ATHENEUM New York 1982 207p

Library of Congress Cataloging in Publication Data

McKillip, Patricia A.
  Stepping from the shadows.

  I. Title.
PS3563.C38S8   1982   813'.54   81-69151
ISBN 0-689-11211-4   AACR2

Published simultaneously in Canada by McClelland and Stewart Ltd.
Composed by American–Stratford Graphic Services, Inc.,
  Brattleboro, Vermont
Manufactured by R. R. Donnelley & Sons Co.,
  Harrisonburg, Virginia
Designed by Mary Cregan
First Edition

for Peter

Stepping from the shadows

you started the hounds baying.
I sat in the field listening to a flute.
You brought a handful of buttercups,
too much color against your dark skin.
You ate one, and
the flute stopped.
So there was only the distant baying of hounds,
hoarse, urgent.
I wanted you to keep coming out of the tree-shadows,
to keep coming always,
bringing with you the distant warnings of hounds.

Stepping from the Shadows

1 ⚞ HELL-GIANTS

The morning air was green. Little speckles of sunlight
floated in front of my eyes. Frances, who was going to get
into trouble, was in the bathroom, telling herself a story.
"Once upon a time," she said to her toes, "there were two
sisters living in a deep dark forest full of alligators. . . ."
I heard my mother from a distance: "Frances, get out of the
bathroom, you'll be late for school!" I banged on the wall
for Frances to stop dreaming. Then I settled back to watch
the motes in the sunlight dance like words in front of my
eyes. Arizona, the sun said. Pizza pie, St. Thomas Aquinas,
beer, Eisenhower, third grade, cactus, God, World War III,
all-together-now:

3

All around the mulberry bush,
The monkey chased the weasel.
That's the way the money goes,
POP—

"Frances!"

The song came bellowing out of the bathroom at the same time as the shout from the kitchen. Frances opened the door. She was barefoot, in her cotton underpants, and I moaned. She was always slow, always dreaming, and I had to nag her just to do things the way ordinary people did.

"You'll make me late for school! Will you hurry up?"

She turned, stood on tiptoe, and leaned over the sink a moment, staring at her plump, quiet face full of freckles, and her two front teeth missing. She whispered, "Pop," and disappeared, so the mirror went blank.

I said, "Hurry up! Get your uniform on! Get your shoes on! Brush your teeth, eat your breakfast—"

"Okay, okay," she said mildly, padding into our bedroom.

"Did you do your arithmetic? Did you learn your catechism questions? Did you say your prayers this morning?"

"Yes, yes, yes," she said. "Shut up." She buttoned her white blouse, then plopped down on the bed with her face in the light. Her eyes closed; she slid one hand under her blouse, touching her nipples. Then she sighed, and her eyes flickered open again to the light.

"Frances!"

"Okay!" she shouted. "Okay, okay, okay, okay . . ." Her voice dwindled; she bent over slowly to pull on her socks.

"You'll get into trouble," I warned her. "You'll get a demerit, and people will laugh."

But she only shook her head a little, sniffing at the smell of oatmeal. "Are there raisins in it?" Then she sang very softly, "All around the mulberry bush . . ."

Finally, she was ready to go. She was still singing as she walked down the sidewalk. The morning was cheerful, and no one was around, so I let her. The blue desert sky was sitting on top of the saguaro cactuses; they were holding it up in their arms. The pleats in Frances's gray uniform jumper were already wrinkling, and her skirt was pinned together since the button had popped off just at the last moment. She was hugging notebooks and schoolbooks—religion, history, spelling, reading—all covered with brown paper from grocery bags. She was squinting a little as she sang; her eyes were going blurry, but no one had discovered it yet. I could see to my own satisfaction: bits of sandstone, quartz, shiny stars of mica scattering the walk from someone's driveway. A lizard panting under a prickly pear. Tar on the telephone pole. In summer, tar on the street got so hot it bubbled and blistered our bare feet. It was spring now. The warm spring rains fell so hard the streets turned into rivers within minutes, and we would stop wading in the gutters to watch the sheet lightning sizzle above the blue mountains. In summer, there were red ants and scorpions. In winter, people's breaths froze in the air, and there were tales of things that happened before we existed, mysteries. . . .

She changed songs, passing Dennis Fish's house.

Three blind mice
See how they run.
They all ran after the farmer's wife,
She cut off their tails with a carving knife,
Did you ever see such a sight in your life?
Three blind mice.

"Who was the farmer's wife?" Frances asked. "Why were the mice blind? Why did they chase the farmer's wife, and what's a carving knife?"

"I don't know," I said. It was a mysterious song, out of the past. She changed songs again to a different language.

Tantum ergo sacramentum,
Veneremur cernui . . .

It had to do with God, incense, and fish. The world was jumbled with language, though it looked very simple: blue sky, houses in a desert, cactus, prairie dog holes, hummingbirds. But against my chest was long division, and beyond the sky were a thousand saints, praying for our souls.

Lupe Ramirez waved as she crossed the street at the corner. The sun paused like a halo behind a great, weatherbeaten saguaro with one green arm pointing heavenward and a hole like an eye in its face where a small bird lived. Lupe Ramirez had tiny gold rings in her ears. They flashed as she stepped off the sidewalk onto the dirt, reminding me of a dream I had when the front wheel of the old tricycle I used to ride went bump and woke me.

"Don't be late!" Lupe shouted. She reached the end of the vacant lot and crossed the road to the dirt hillock ringing the schoolyard, keeping kickballs from rolling out of it, rolling across the small wilderness of jumping cactus, yucca trees, and rattlesnakes, and across the gas station lot at the other end of the world where we bought Necco wafers and Tootsie Rolls, and across the city, and up to the blue secret mountains where the lightning began. Lupe's body ascended the dirt hillock and disappeared.

The eight o'clock bell rang from the church. The bird hid in the cactus; the sun moved to attention above the cross on the school. A door slammed at the end of the block. Kelly Teague ran out, dropped her books all over the lawn, and kicked the garbage can at the end of the drive. It bonged, but it was full of garbage, so it didn't move very much. She was still kicking it when we came.

"My brother makes me so mad." The can bonged again. Her fists were clenched, and her face, which reminded me of an acorn with pale hair, was pinched. "He ate all the Sugar Smacks, so I had to eat cornflakes. He copied my homework; then he drew a face on it—I'm going to punch his eye out."

"Then you won't be twins anymore," Frances said.

"We're not twins."

"Yes, you are."

"No, we're not. I hate him. It's not fair having to be twins with someone you hate." There was a shout from inside the house; her foot froze in midair, dropped reluctantly. She whirled, stamped back toward the house. "At least you get to eat all the Sugar Smacks by yourself," she yelled back before the screen door slammed behind her again. I stood still a moment, looking at Kelly's spilled books. Frances began to sing again, very softly, reminding me she was there, and we started walking again.

The jackrabbits had come out at night in the vacant lot, leaving their droppings like a dot-to-dot game all over the dirt. Frances veered suddenly. It seemed impossible to keep her moving in a straight line, out of trouble. She followed a trail of droppings over to a clump of tumbleweeds and thistles that shouldn't have been rustling. She peeked behind it and found Dennis Fish. I thought he was eating his lunch, but he was eating from a little pile of sand. He gulped when he saw Frances. He had a milky face with freckles all over it and bright red hair in a butch. Frances squatted down, gazing at him.

"What are you doing? Why don't you eat breakfast?"

He shrugged a little, listlessly. He was thin, but he always moved as if he had no bones under his pale skin. His face looked upset. "That's weird," I said. "Eating sand. You're weird."

"I like it." His voice was a cross between a whine and a croak. He handed Frances a little plastic ice-cream spoon. "Try it." He brushed a little at the hole he had dug. "Down there where it's damp."

Frances scraped at the bottom of the hole. She took a spoonful of sand, held it a moment in her mouth, then swallowed. Dennis watched her hopefully.

"Do you like it?"

"Crunchy." She coughed a grain up, then swallowed it. "It's kind of cool and dark. I thought it would taste like worms."

"You're going to get worms or something, eating from Dennis's spoon. You'll get weird, too," I said, but she ignored me. She gave Dennis back the spoon and glanced at the alcove of tumbleweeds.

8

"Is this your secret place?"

"Only this morning. The tumbleweeds'll blow away." He added, poking at the sand, "I have lots of secret places."

"Why?"

His face was growing closed, but he answered anyway. "Everyone laughs at me. So I find places to go. And my mom doesn't like me."

"She's got to like you."

"No, she doesn't."

"Yes, she does."

"She doesn't. She says I must have fallen off the moon because she's never seen anyone like me."

"The moon." Frances's chin descended to her bent knees as she studied him; her hands played with her shoelaces. I thought of Dennis Fish on the moon. It would be a secret place: silent, shadowless, colorless like his skin.

"What was it like?"

"I didn't fall off the damn moon!" he shouted aggrievedly.

"Your mother said you did. She would know."

"I didn't," he said, but without conviction. He dug out another spoonful of sand. Frances stood up, and his face lifted quickly, pleading. "Frances. Don't tell anyone I fell off the moon. They'll laugh."

"I won't," she promised. The warning bell rang then, and Dennis grabbed at his books. We ran, books joggling in our arms, broke through the first graders, and slid home in the third-grade line just as Dan and Kelly Teague came panting behind us.

We sang "The Star-Spangled Banner" to Father Malachi. Then we filed inside and saluted God, His kingdom come, His will be done, and the flag, under God, indivisible, with liberty and daily bread for all. Sister Thomas Augustine had taught us many things: how there were forty-nine states and nine choirs of angels, how the decimals could be moved in long division, and how a soul could be moved through our prayers from the loneliness of purgatory to the bliss of heaven. How Nathan Hale had died for our country and Christ had died for our sins. Seven rows of bodies dusted their knees off after praying and sat down in seven rows of desks. All the shoulders were white; all the feet sticking out were white. Only Keith MacIntyre's desk was empty. I watched it awhile; then something Sister Thomas Augustine was saying began to creep into my mind.

". . . He lives in the shadow of darkness upon the earth and in the terrible fires of hell. He takes many forms of evil, and you must always guard against him. If you get angry or don't want to obey your parents, that's Satan, whispering in your ear, trying to pull you away from God's grace into sin." Sister Thomas Augustine was small, with crooked teeth and a cheerful smile, though she wasn't smiling then. Only her hands and face showed. The rest of her was hidden behind black skirts, black veils, and shoes, a stiff white bib and white band over her forehead to keep her heart and mind pure. "Your purpose on earth is to serve God and live in perfect happiness with Him when you die. But God permits Satan to test us, and because of that, we have great evils in the world—murders, faithlessness, wars—when men listen to Satan rather than God." The whole class was still in front of her. My arms were prickling, and I began to listen for a whispering beneath the air. Dan Teague stuck his hand up.

"What does he look like, Ster?"

"He is a fallen angel, once the most beautiful of angels, and his name meant 'light.' But he sinned against God, and lost his beauty, and fell from heaven. In earlier times, men drew him as a snake or as a winged man with horns and cloven hooves, like a goat. But no one really knows. So be good, children. Be very, very good."

She paused, allowing us time to think about our sins. George Barnes, who was fat and breathed funny, wanted to know how hot hell was. "Very hot." Was it hot as a stove burner? Hot as a barbecue fire? Hot as the desert in summer, when the air was an oven and the ground burned your feet? My thoughts drifted away. Hot was hot. Another question puzzled me. I watched a horned angel in my mind fall from light into fire. Satan had fallen from heaven. Dennis Fish had fallen off the moon. Where had I come from?

Sister Thomas Augustine's voice faded. There was an open door beside her. It was a square of wood, and within the wood was a living world of dust and green cactus and blue sky. The gold striking out of the sky made me want to remember something I had forgotten . . . something older than my first pair of patent-leather shoes, older than my great-grandmother feeding the pigs in Oregon, older than the door shutting softly in the night and waking me. . . . Where was I before that? Before there were words and numbers and saints. When there was only the hot earth and the sky, and I had no name. Where was I? I wanted to know suddenly. I needed to know. Where was I when the sun existed before I did? The desert outside was old, old;

even heaven and hell were old. I was something new in an old world, and I did not know why.

I heard voices again, slowly; Sister Thomas Augustine was asking catechism questions. I knew them so well I could have stood and answered them one after another without being asked. Who made you? God made me. Why did God make you? God made me to know, love, and serve Him, and be happy with Him forever in heaven. Who is God? God is the Supreme Being who made all things. He dwelt among the cactus and the rattlesnakes; He gave His only begotten son unto the world, who hung crucified between the clock and the map of Arizona. Sister Thomas Augustine's voice interrupted me, asking a question. Frances stood up, answered, and sat down again. Sister Thomas Augustine's voice dragged her back up.

"Do you know, Frances," she asked, "that you gave exactly the right answer to a question I haven't asked yet?"

Frances sat down again, staring at her desk top. Her face was fiery behind her freckles. The class was laughing at her, and I was angry because she did such a stupid thing. Then I forgot about the laughter. I kept watching myself grow smaller and smaller in my mind, as far back as I could remember. I knew we all were part of God's eternal plan, but it bothered me that I could find nothing beyond my memories except nothing.

"Frances Stuart!"

I jumped. Somehow numbers had appeared on the blackboard. Frances was blinking at them fuzzily, and I sighed. She couldn't see. She couldn't do even that right.

"Yes, Ster?"

"Well, don't just sit there daydreaming. Go up and solve the problem."

It was long division. Frances went up the aisle slowly, one hand over the pin in her skirt. Somehow, while the class waited for her, she got chalk dust all over her face and hands. She found one answer, but when she tried to check it with multiplication, it wasn't the same answer. She stood there staring at the blackboard, blinking at the different answers. I put my fingers over my eyes. A bird sang outside. And suddenly I was outside with the bird in the blue sky, flying to my home high inside a saguaro and making the only sound in the world.

"Dan Teague." Sister sighed. "Go help Frances with her problem. Frances, there is no need to cry."

She always cried when things went wrong, big, silent, exasperating tears in front of everyone. No one else did that; she was always embarrassing me, making me angry with her. Lupe passed her a Kleenex so she could mix the tears and chalk dust around on her face. Dan couldn't do the problem right either, in spite of his grin. Finally, Michael Sayers stepped to the board and worked the problems with a few deft flicks of chalk. I wondered if his bright white teeth had anything to do with being good at arithmetic. With God, Sister Thomas Augustine said, all things are possible.

The long morning wore into noon. We sat outside under the shadow of the Virgin Mary, who was smiling at the Arizona sun: Dan and Kelly Teague, Dennis Fish, Lupe Ramirez, Frances and I. I found a sandwich and tomatoes in my lunch, but no cookies. Dennis Fish was chewing a peanut-butter sandwich and discussing World War III. His face looked round, solemn with importance, in the shadow more moonlike than ever.

"The TV said it might start any day now," he said. "I told Sister Thomas Augustine. She says we have to pray, and if the Russians bomb us, we have to crawl under our desks. Or if we're in the playground, we have to find a place to hide."

"The church," Lupe suggested. "God wouldn't let them bomb a church. Not a Catholic church."

"They're Russians," Dan Teague said briefly. "They'll bomb what they want. And we won't have time to run; we'll be wiped out before we know it. Just a flash of light and—" He made the sound of a bomb exploding. Then he angled his hands and imitated a machine gun blowing off the smiling head of the Blessed Virgin.

"Don't," Lupe said, shocked. I pulled a piece of memory out of the dark places of my mind.

"My father was in a war," I said slowly, "when I was little."

"He was not," Dan said. "There wasn't one."

"There was," Frances said. I let her talk because she was right for once and she was better at remembering. "My mother was ironing, and he was gone. I asked her where he was, and she said he was at war."

"What war?"

"I don't know."

"There wasn't one," he said, but without conviction.

Lupe asked suddenly, "Where is Russia?"

"Everywhere," Dan Teague said ominously. "Like hell."

"It is not," Kelly argued. "I asked Ster. She said it was

down there." She pointed to the grass. "Under the earth." She stripped open a bag of potato chips with her teeth. Dan grabbed them away from her and danced out of reach. I wondered how they could be twins when he was so big and dark. "Da-an!" She bounced off the grass, her foot poised to kick. "DanTeaguegivemebackmypotatochips! I'm going to kill you."

He backed against the pedestal, one hand on the Blessed Virgin's foot, which was stepping on a snake's head. "You'll go to hell."

"You stole my potato chips! So will you!"

He eluded her outstretched hands and swung himself higher up the pedestal. Lupe said objectively, "Stealing potato chips is only a venial sin. Killing is a mortal sin. Your soul will be black as a milk bottle."

Kelly aimed a kick but only stubbed her toe on the pedestal. "A what?" she gasped.

"There are three milk bottles—"

"Where?" Dan hoisted himself farther up. His knees were at Kelly's chin; she pummeled at them futilely while he poured chips into his mouth.

"On the blackboard. Listen. Your soul is like three milk bottles. If you commit a mortal sin, your soul is empty of milk, and you go to hell, unless you go to confession. If you commit a venial sin, like spitting on the church steps, your soul is like a milk bottle with little black dots, half full of grace. And after you go to confession, it is all full of milk, white as—"

"Look what Dan's sitting on," Dennis interrupted with fascinated horror. "It's the devil."

Dan looked down. His rear end was cradled in the snake's

coils; he held its neck with one hand. A stone mouth twisted to hiss soundlessly at him. He crunched potato chips audibly and jumped down. Kelly's kick caught him square on the shin; he grunted and fell on the grass, scattering chips all over.

"Serves you right," Kelly said furiously. Frances was still staring at the snake. Then somebody bopped my head with a spelling book, and she closed her mouth. A dark gypsy face came over the sun; it made me smile.

"Hi, Keith."

"Hi, Fran-Anne." He dropped down among the chips and popped a few in his mouth. Dan sat up, holding his shin with both hands.

"You're going to catch holy hell," he said with awe.

Keith shrugged. "I know." He had black hair and eyes and muscles like wires in his arms. He flunked tests and picked his scars in class, making girls squeal. Frances never flunked tests, but she liked him for some reason.

She said, "Where were you? How come you're so late?"

"Ah—things." He shrugged again, moodily, then tossed his book in the air and caught it. "I had to get my brother out of a tree. He climbed up naked and wouldn't come down. My mom finally called the firemen."

Even Dan's mouth was open. "You don't think Ster will believe that."

Keith produced a piece of dirty paper. "She wrote me a note. It's all here." The bell rang then, and we got up and trailed him into class to see more excitement. But there wasn't much. Sister Thomas Augustine only read the note, closed her eyes, and sighed.

"Lord, give me patience," she murmured. "Hand in your

arithmetic if you've done it, and sit down. Your brother is a demon in disguise."

After recess we had geography, and Michael Sayers talked about Scotland. I watched his teeth and tried to pay attention. But my feet kept shifting. I watched a bug crawl across the floor. I watched the sun shift over the map of Arizona to touch the silver body of Christ. His arms and the clock's hands were crucified in the same angle: ten minutes to two. He had made the sun; it glinted off the nails in His palms. He had made me. He had come to earth as a man, hung on a cross, and died. Then He had risen again with the morning. In winter He had been born; in spring He had died, on Good Friday. On Easter morning He walked across the earth again softly as a wind. He had caught fish for His disciples and cooked them breakfast. Then He had risen into the stars, where He dwelt with angels and saints. If I served Him perfectly, I would rise to the stars also when I died. It was very simple. Mass on Sundays and holy days; fish on Fridays and during Lent; obey your parents, your teachers, priests, and the Pope. Don't lie, cheat, steal, blaspheme, or despair. Visit the sick, bury the dead, love your neighbor as yourself, and, above all, love God, who was crowned with thorns, whose hands were full of light. Who was hated by a snake, by a man with horns, who had fallen like a bright star out of heaven, who wanted to pull us all—Dan and Kelly Teague, Dennis Fish, even Sister Thomas Augustine—out of the clear sunlight into his fire.

Sister Thomas Augustine's voice startled me. Frances was getting into trouble again for daydreaming. I gritted my teeth, hoping she wouldn't cry. It was bad enough that her face wasn't very pretty; she didn't have to blotch it with tears. But she only swallowed several times and sat very still, her shoulders hunched a little under Sister's words. Finally, Sister turned away, and I felt a hand on my shoulder.

"Never mind," Keith whispered across the aisle. "Ster Thomas Augustine's a stupid bitch."

I froze, watching for the lightning to char him to cinders in his seat. But God waited.

Finally, the last bell rang. I wanted to yell at Frances for being so embarrassing to me, but Lupe caught up with me as we clattered out.

"What are you going to confess at your first confession?" she asked.

I thought blankly. "Everything, I guess. Why?"

She stepped closer to me as we crossed the schoolyard. It was dusty since we hadn't had rain for three weeks, and little dust devils were whirling around us. I watched them, wondering why I found them strange in a world full of so many strange things.

"I can't think of anything," Lupe said. She sounded close to tears. "I'm too busy helping take care of Mikie and Maria to think. What am I going to tell Father Healy when I'm in the confessional and he asks me what I've done wrong?"

The tetherball chains clanked as the balls spun wildly. First graders linked hands, giggling as they circled. "Ring around the rosie, pocket full of posies, ashes, ashes, we all fall *down!*" We passed second graders jumping rope with little spurts of dust; the rope swished up, down, and tangled in the jumper's feet. Other little kids were filing under an arch of arms and chanting:

London Bridge is falling down, falling down, falling down, London Bridge is falling down, my fair lady O!

"Well," I said, "you could go commit a few sins before then. Spit at somebody. Or Keith knows a lot of bad words."

"I couldn't," she breathed.

"Just one. Whisper it. Wait—there he is. I'll ask him."

"I can't," she wailed, but I grabbed Keith's arm as he bounced a kickball out to the playing field.

"Keith, Lupe needs some sins. Teach her a bad word."

He looked at us a moment, a curious, tired expression on his face. "Shit," he said. "I've got something better. I can tell you where babies come from."

We both were silent. Lupe looked a little startled. "Is that a sin?"

"It is if you're not married."

I felt bewildered. "Babies come out of a mother's stomach."

"But do you know how they get in there?"

"It's something to do with being married."

"No," he said. "It has to do with sex. Wait—" His muscles tensed as someone yelled to him; he bounced the ball once and sent it in a flying kick toward a group of boys. "I'll tell you later. I got to go—later tonight."

We watched him lope across the yard, catching up with the ball. Lupe's face was puckered. "What's he talking about? My mother had six babies and she never said anything about sex."

I couldn't answer. Something was pushing into my mind, something I had seen, before a door shut, and I didn't want my eyes to see it again. It was secret, it was hidden; no one spoke of it, yet it was there, pushing into my head. Lupe murmured something about babies and left me, but I couldn't speak. I stood, trying to get away from the thought, while all the sounds dwindled around me, and then I heard Frances's voice suddenly, freeing me, pulling me back into the world where people didn't think what I was thinking.

"Why are you standing here daydreaming?"

"I'm not," I said furiously. It felt better to be angry. "You're the one who daydreams. Can't you get through one day without getting into trouble? Just one day? Look at you! Your shoes are a mess, your skirt's a mess, you look funny with no teeth—Dan Teague laughs at you. You answer questions before they're asked, you can't do long division, you can't see straight—"

"Shut up," she said, but very softly because she knew I was right.

"Your voice is soft, your face is soft, your name is soft, everything in you is soft, you can hardly even kick a kick-ball."

Her head was bowed; she was hugging her books against her tightly. She sniffed, blinking down at the ground, but she didn't cry. Dust drifted between us, across her shadow. She was waiting for me to speak.

Finally, I confessed. "I saw something, and then a door closed, and I don't know what I saw. I mean—I know what I saw, but I don't know why it's so terrible that it's not even on the list of sins Father Healy gave us to be forgiven. Are there things that can't be forgiven?"

She lifted her head slowly then, looking at the blue above
the red tiles on the school roof. "Yes. Lots of things." She
moved finally, scuffling, turning her white shoes even dust-
ier. Her voice rose a little. "Lots."

After supper, after we had jumped rope and played hop-
scotch on the sidewalk and watched "The Mouseketeers"
and "The Lone Ranger" and pretended we had done our
homework, we ran outside again. The sun was just about
to set. Long black shadows from telephone poles and cactuses shot across the ground. Dan and Keith were throwing
a softball on the street. We called to them. Lupe came
running down the street, with her older brother Carlos.
Lisa Silverman, who was Jewish and never had to go to
church on Sundays, came out of her house across the street.
We played hide-and-seek. Dennis Fish came out to join
us; we made him "It." He hid his face against a tree and
counted very fast while we scrambled for hiding places over
fences, behind bushes and garbage pails, inside garages. The
sun set slowly, burning down into the clouds; the sky went
orange and red, then darkened slowly into soft blue-gray
twilight. Our shadows disappeared from under our feet. It
got too dusky for hide-and-seek. We played tag awhile, then
freeze, on the lawn. It was nearly dark. Only the light
from the open doors and windows of the houses showed
us what statues we became. We wrestled, somersaulted,
twisted ourselves into weird shapes until Keith shouted,
"Freeze!" and we became statues, without voices, without
faces. Keith walked slowly among us. Dennis Fish stared
at him with his head between his legs. Kelly had her hands

flat on the ground, one foot lifted for the beginning of a cartwheel. No one moved. No one even giggled. Frances was in a dumb position, squatting down like a frog with her chin on one knee. Lupe was standing on one leg with her arms outstretched. Keith touched her hand. She came alive slowly, blinking. Then he touched me, and I straightened.

"All right," he said. "Now listen."

He talked very softly and steadily for a couple of moments. Lupe seemed perplexed when he finished.

"You mean little Mikie's tinkler? All he does is mess up his diapers with it."

"He'll grow."

"But, Keith, do people really do that?"

"My mother does it all the time."

I was remembering. I heard a sound, touched a door very slowly, so that it moved silently, silently, until the dark cracked open in front of my eye. My father was going to the bathroom. I saw his white flank and something else, half familiar, half secret, that grew between his legs. He didn't want me to see. He reached out to the door, saying nothing. He left me standing in the empty hall, alone with my secret, with the door shut gently, firmly in my face.

"All right," Keith said patiently. "Try saying 'fuck.'"

But the terrible word shocked us both into statues again.

Our parents called us in finally, voices coming from both ends of the block. Frances was very quiet. After we went to bed, I read with a flashlight out of an old *Grimm's Fairy Tales* book with odd, squiggly illustrations in it. I whispered to Frances about the twelve dancing sisters, and their night world with leaves of jewels, and the most beautiful of the princesses who was rewarded with the prince. But she still couldn't speak, and I was afraid of what was in her head. She woke me with her screaming in the middle of the night. When I finally blinked into the light, she was sitting in the bathroom on Father's knee, while Mother washed her face with a warm cloth.

"Sh," Mother said. "Sh. You were dreaming, honey, you had a bad dream."

She sniffled, recognizing the real world. Father drew her wet, tangled hair out of her eyes. "It's all right, now. You're awake." He smelled comfortingly of sleep and cigarette smoke. His hair was mussed; he had the expression on his face that reminded me of the picture of Christ with the children on his dresser. "What were you dreaming? Must have been pretty frightening."

She gazed at him, remembering, then shook her head surprisedly. "No." Her voice croaked. "There wasn't anything scary."

"Then why were you crying like that?"

"I don't know. It's just the same dream I always have. It's not scary."

"Then why do you cry like that? You scared us."

"I don't know."

"You open a door," she whispered later in the dark, trying to understand. "There's a big underground cave, with enormous tree roots sticking down into it. And boys— like Keith—playing in the dirt under the roots. They live there; they're having fun—"

"Is that what makes you cry?"

"No. Farther down in the cave, there's a train track, with some train cars open on it. One of them has its side doors open. And some men are trying to push something long and really big into the train car, but the car is too narrow, the thing won't go. . . . Then I feel this wet washcloth on my face, and I open my eyes, and I'm in the bathroom, and I don't even know I've been crying. . . . It doesn't make any sense." Her voice was fading. "It wasn't scary. So why do I cry? I'm always crying . . . except when I'm in the dream. . . ."

The next morning, as we walked to school, we found Keith in the vacant lot, kneeling in front of his brother, who was in his underwear.

"Please," Keith was begging. "Please."

"Uhh-uhh," said the child. Frances stopped. I let her since I was curious, too.

"What's wrong?" Keith's little brother was a legend, like a saint, only the nuns said he was a little devil.

"He ran away from home," Keith said disgustedly.

"What for?" Frances hunched down beside them in the dirt, fascinated. Nobody ran away from home, least of all in his underwear.

"I don't know. He wouldn't eat his Cream of Wheat, he wouldn't get dressed—Johnny! I'll drag you, I swear it—"

"Uhh-uhh." Johnny was skinny, pale, and spidery without his clothes. He had flat, fearless gray eyes and the dirtiest morning face I had ever seen. Keith stood over him, baffled, his fists opening and closing. But the child's eyes only glinted mockingly at his uniform.

"Where's he running to?"

"I don't know," Keith said wearily. "He's done this before. I have to get him home. She can't control him." The slight jerk of his head toward his house told me who "she" was. The tone of his voice startled me. "She says he's a wild child."

The Wild Child smiled faintly. Frances stared at him, pouring a handful of dust over her shoe. She hadn't talked much all morning; she had been slower than usual, yawning between pulls at her socks. Keith scowled darkly at his brother.

"God damn it—"

I jumped, but the Wild Child only said instantly, "Uhh-uhh."

Keith pushed dirty hands through his hair. Then he touched me. "You'd better go. You'll be late."

"So will you."

"I have to get him home."

"You'll get a tardy slip. You'll get a demerit."

"I don't care." But he did. "You go on. Go on, Frances. I'll hurry."

Frances rose slowly, her eyes on the unrepentent, faintly smiling eyes of the Wild Child. The bell rang, and she started. I sighed and ran for it, as always.

Sister Thomas Augustine was crosser than usual. She threw an eraser across the room at Dan when he turned around to talk to Michael; she snapped at Karen Goodwater, who wore red satin bows in her hair and never did anything wrong. She got mad at Dennis Fish when he couldn't answer his catechism questions; Dennis's milky face went bright red until I thought he was going to cry. Then Sister asked Frances a question, and Frances, staring off into space, didn't hear her.

"What am I going to do with you, child?" Sister demanded. "What am I going to do? How are you going to get through life if you can't pay attention to the world around you? You do know there is a world out here, Frances, don't you?"

Frances turned into a snail, trying to disappear inside herself while Sister yelled at her. I just wished she would disappear completely, change into someone else, who never dreamed, never had buttons pop off her skirt, and always had the right answer at the right time. Then Michael Sayers, who was playing with a rubber band, snapped it accidentally across the room, hitting Karen in the arm and distracting Sister Thomas Augustine. Frances was still trying to vanish down her blouse. Then I saw something that made me forget about her. Beyond the open door, beyond the schoolyard, the Wild Child was running through the patch of desert in his underwear. He disappeared among the cactuses, and a tiny Keith moved into view, stopped. He cupped his hands to his mouth and shouted.

"Children!"

We stopped whispering, shuffling, and snickering at Michael. Sister Thomas Augustine had a sheaf of papers in her hand. She looked grim, and we became very still.

"You will be making your first confession in two weeks and your first holy communion in a month. Yet every one of you except Karen Goodwater and Lupe Ramirez flunked your last religion test." She paused to let that sink in. There was not a sound in the room. "There is no excuse for that. I'm very, very disappointed in you, and I'm sure God must be, too." She began to move around the room. A paper floated onto my desk. I heard her voice a moment later. "Even you, Frances. I'm surprised at you."

There were red slashes all over the paper and a big red F at the top. I closed my eyes and still saw it. I had never gotten one before. The name was mine, the printing was mine, but all the answers were wrong. I had flunked original sin, the seven deadly sins, the three cardinal virtues, and the act of contrition. If I opened my eyes, I would see a pair of silvery feet with a nail driven through them. You are to be perfect, the crucified God had said. Even as your Heavenly Father is perfect. I had played hide-and-seek instead of studying that night. And carelessness, Sister Thomas Augustine said, was the hammer that drove the nails into the wood.

I couldn't even cry; I could only let out a little air in a sigh. The beautiful, horned angel was already tugging at my soul. I didn't hear Sister talk for the next ten minutes. I heard the recess bell dimly and the subdued murmurings around me. I couldn't find Frances anywhere; she had left me. I got up slowly, feeling as though I were walking into a dream. The dream took me out of the classroom, across the schoolyard grass, away from the school and the church toward the desert.

I followed a line of jackrabbit spoor past the volleyball games, tetherball games, jump rope, kickball teams. The droppings continued up the mound of dirt that served as the schoolyard boundary until Father Healy could afford a steel fence. I climbed over it and crossed the dusty road into the desert. I found Keith by the sound of his voice, and sat down beside him in a circle of prickly pears.

"I flunked my religion test," I said, and he whirled.

"What are you doing here?" His voice was hoarse; it squealed a little in astonishment. I hugged my knees tight against my heart.

"I flunked my religion test."

"You never flunk tests."

"I flunked it."

He slid both his hands through his hair and sat down beside me. His white uniform blouse had dusty handprints all over it. "You're going to get into trouble. You can't just walk out of school."

"I don't care."

He was silent a moment, just breathing. Finally, he said, "If you flunked it, I flunked it. Did I?"

"Yes." He sighed, and I added, "Everybody did. Except Karen and Lupe."

"Fuck."

"Keith—" I breathed.

"Ah, well." He flung a rock at the nose of a lizard living under a cactus, and it flicked back into its hole. "I'm probably going to hell anyway. Especially after I kill Johnny."

I looked at him out of the corners of my eyes. "You can't," I said. "It's a mortal sin."

He looked down, picked at a scar on his wrist. I watched listlessly. His grades were bad, and he was always in trouble, but he was usually cheerful, good-natured in spite of it. He wiped at his nose with the back of his hand and patted my shoulder.

"I'll bury him out here, where no one will find him. You go back to school."

"No. You can't kill your own brother."

28

"Why not? He'll be burned raw anyway, running around all day with nothing on but his underpants. Stupid kid. Dumb, stupid, goddamned kid." He stood up restlessly, shouting. "Johnny! If I find you, I'm going to throw you right in the middle of the biggest jumping cactus I can find!" He was silent, listening. I stopped breathing. A wind puffed across the trail, dragging a sheet of dust between us and the schoolyard. Recess had ended; the schoolyard was still again. There was no sound but the desert wind. The dust veered over us suddenly, passed away. The round stubby heads of barrel cactus, the angled fingers of jumping cactus that grabbed at you and clung reappeared. Keith shambled tiredly after the dust; I got up and followed him until we could no longer see the houses or the school. Then a mocking laugh echoed down the wind, and Keith's fists clenched.

"Johnneeee!" He ran toward it, dodging saguaros and yucca trees. Dust blew between us, filling my eyes, making my nose run. I had a stitch in my side, and I was afraid of the gropings of the jumping cactuses. The sky was so hot it was pale, and I could feel the heat of the ground under my feet. I saw prairie dog holes, but no prairie dogs, only lizards, flicking their tongues as they scurried away from me. Keith slowed finally, winded. He grabbed a rock and flung it as hard as he could. It bounced off the flank of a saguaro with one great twisted arm pointing downward to the fiery earth. The cactus seemed to jeer at him suddenly, in a distant, high-pitched voice.

"Can't catch me. Can't . . ." It faded. Keith swore, tensed, breathing furiously. Then he threw himself down on the ground. Our shadows looked black and crisp, shriveled like bacon. There was a piece of skull where Keith had dropped; he picked it up listlessly, examined the teeth. Then he rolled over onto his back. His face lay in the shadow of a barrel cactus. That reassured me. If we were lost in the desert, we could cut it open to find water. We could even eat it if we were lost too long. I touched one of the thorns. They were long and curved, like fishhooks. It seemed a secret thing, as if underneath the green surface full of fishhooks it were busy thinking. My mind was thinking, too: strange, dreamlike thoughts that didn't have anything to do with what was true or real. But in the desert, with Keith, I felt safe, so I let them come. Maybe the cactus was only blind and mouthless by day. Or maybe it was a giant thumb tip poking out of the earth. There were giants buried under the earth, with only their thumbs sticking out and their fingers, which were the saguaros. I wondered what their faces were like. They would be green Hell-Giants, since hell was beneath the earth. Keith's voice woke me.

"Don't go to sleep. It's dangerous to sleep in the desert."

"Cowboys do it all the time," I said drowsily.

"Only at night."

"Doesn't he even care that he's running around in his underpants? What if somebody sees him?"

"He doesn't care. He hates his uniform. Ster Agatha says he's the worst first grader she's ever had. He won't sit still; he won't pray; he swears; he eats his lunch during class. He won't even try to learn to read or spell. He just laughs. He's crazy." He sighed at the sky, then dropped his wrist over his eyes. "He runs out at night, too, if Mom

30

doesn't watch him. One night I snuck out late, and I tripped over him on the front lawn."

"What was he doing?"

"Nothing. Just looking at the moon. Staring at it, like a wild animal. He's nuts. He has great dreams, though. He'll wake up in the morning and tell me sometimes . . . all full of colors, and beautiful places, planets, stars. . . . He's happy then, sitting there stark naked, telling his dreams. . . . He doesn't believe in pajamas. It's lucky he had even his underpants on when he got away from me. One morning I found him sitting naked in the snapdragons." He made a grunt like a laugh. Then he added, "He never cries. Mom spanks him until she's worn-out, but he never cries."

I was silent, poking a stick into a hump of ground full of ants. There were rattlesnakes, scorpions, gila monsters, dangerous things all around us. I didn't know what time it was; the hot, shimmering air had been there forever. Keith stirred.

"I've got to find him. Got to bring him back before dark. He'll get bitten by a rattler; he'll fall in a cactus. . . ." He gathered himself up slowly. A rock hit the ground where he had been lying, and he jumped.

"Damn you! You freaky little SOB, I'll scalp you!"

He ran again, and I panted after him. I wanted him to catch the Wild Child; I wanted to hear his dreams. I was too tired to keep up; Keith was well ahead of me when he tangled with something that had stepped in front of him. I thought it was Johnny, and I hurried before he slipped away. But it was only Dennis Fish.

He was snuffling when I came up. "Hi. I saw you leave at recess and come here. Can I do whatever it is you're doing?"

Keith shrugged a little, running his hands through his hair. "Hell," he said tiredly. "I thought you were my brother. That's why I tackled you. I'm going to kill him."

"Ump," Dennis said. He was too upset to be impressed. All his books lay on the ground; he didn't move to pick them up. "What's the use of anything? I try, and try, and try, and all I do is flunk things, and my dad yells at me." His eyes were red, and his skin beneath his freckles was very white. He added, "Or he yells at my mom. I'm tired. I can't even see the numbers on the blackboard anymore, hardly. So Ster yells at me for that."

"I can't see either," I said. I patted his back a little since he looked so miserable. "Must be like your teeth falling out. Your eyes change, too, except they forgot to tell us."

"You can't either?" he said. I could tell it made him feel better. "And you flunked your religion test."

"Uh-huh."

"So did I," Keith said. He threw another rock. "And I lost my brother."

"Is he in his underwear?" Dennis pointed. "I saw him running that way."

So we ran again. I shouted to Dennis about his books in the dirt behind us, but he pretended not to hear. I had flunked my religion test, sneaked out of school, and now I was chasing a Wild Child all over a desert, listening to more evil language than I had ever heard in my life. I was probably going to hell. Maybe, judging from the heat, I

32

was already there. It seemed certainly easier to get to than
heaven. And at least, I thought comfortingly, Keith could
be there with me, and we both could see what the fallen
angel looked like. Dust devils were beginning to spin around
us, taller than we were, stalking the Wild Child. The
shadows were getting longer; I was very hungry. But ahead
of us I heard a voice dodging among the cactuses, calling
Keith, wanting him and running from him. I panted on,
the stitch boring into my side. Finally, I couldn't run any
longer. I collapsed under a giant saguaro and lay listening
to my heartbeat. I didn't know where I was; I didn't care.
Ants crawled one by one over my ankle, and I didn't care.
The wind breathed and fell quiet and breathed again. The
cactus shadow lay like a hand across my back. Things moved
around me, but I didn't care. I dreamed a little, of Johnny
whirling like a dust devil through beautiful, secret places.
He could see. He didn't have to know long division. He
could talk to the cactus. Voices called into my dreaming;
he only laughed at them. He could fly. He could reach
out and pick a star like a flower out of the night sky. . . .
Then I saw him crucified on a great saguaro cactus, crying
for Keith, for water, and I woke up, making a noise. I was
dying of thirst.

Lupe Ramirez was sitting beside me, watching me. It
was late; the sun was setting, and her earrings twinkled
wildly.

"What are you doing here?" My voice croaked like a frog.
She shrugged.

"I got tired. Mikie was crying, Maria was crying, Jaimie
was crying, Louisa ripped up the funny papers, Jaimie

33

scribbled all over my homework with a blue crayon. I got tired." There were little smudges of dark under her eyes. "And my mother is going to have another one."

"One what?"

"Baby. You were crying in your dreams."

"I know." I sat still a moment, waiting for my body to wake up. I heard a new pair of voices calling Johnny. "That's Dan and Kelly."

"They thought you were playing a new game. Sister Thomas Augustine couldn't find you anywhere. She was going to call your parents—"

"Ohhh," I sighed.

"Then Father Healy came in and talked to us about our religion test. I think she forgot. He said the world is becoming very dangerous, and he was sad that we were so careless of our religion. He said we are very, very close to World War III, and we must keep our souls very pure, always in a state of grace, to be always prepared for death. Kelly started to cry." She drew her knees up under her chin and hugged them. "Mikie can't even walk without his diapers falling off. How could he run from the bombs?" She sighed. "It's hard to have to worry about so much." She lifted her head then, and her face brightened. "Look at the sun."

It was setting in a pool of fire. The clouds misted white, gold, red, away from it, stretching halfway across the sky, all the colors of the desert. It drew us up; we walked toward it without speaking. The cactuses danced around us in strange, stumpy shapes. The sun slipped farther and farther away from us, burning into blue light, into a secret land beyond the earth, full of colors and mysteries. The faster we walked, the farther it lay. Finally, the shadows faded into dusk, and only a rim of light showed us where the mystery lay.

We heard voices again and drifted toward them. Keith, running, stopped as he reached us.

"I saw him—I saw him. So close I almost had him. We've almost got him cornered. Dan's helping." He flashed away again, and we ran after him, calling. Lupe and I got separated; our calls got farther and farther apart. I saw Dennis run by; his face looked dusty and happy, no longer moonlike. Kelly Teague waved at me as she passed. Dan got jumped by a cactus; I saw him shake a piece of it out of his thumb, then suck it. He grinned at me. Then we both saw the Wild Child, flickering palely over a pile of rocks, and we ran after him, shouting. Dusk turned into twilight; it was hard to tell one shadow from another. Finally, I heard Keith bellow, "I've got you! I've got you, you little—" and Lupe shrieked. We ran toward them and fell over one another. When we sorted ourselves out finally, Frances was with us.

"God damn it," Keith whispered. "God damn it. Where is he? He'll freeze. He hasn't eaten all day." He dropped to the ground, still muttering. I was glad Frances was there. We all sat down wearily among the cactuses. It was growing very dark; I couldn't see the color of anyone's hair. It was past suppertime. I thought if I listened very hard, I might hear all our parents' voices, calling us home. But I heard only the twilight wind.

"Maybe he'll go home in the dark," Kelly said.

"Maybe," Keith said. But he didn't move. None of us moved. We listened to each other breathe. Keith's voice came out of the dark again. "He won't go home. Wait till the moon rises. We'll find him then, staring at it."

"We're going to get into trouble," Kelly said. She slapped at something, then was quiet again.

"My mama will have to feed all the kids by herself," Lupe said. She was next to me, but her face was so dark I couldn't even see her earrings.

I heard Dennis whisper, "I don't care."

"We could live here," Dan said suddenly. "When the war comes. We could hide for the rest of our lives. Build houses out of cactus, eat prickly pears, jackrabbits, rattlesnakes."

"War." Kelly sighed. In the desert she forgot to be angry with him. They were lying close together in the dark. "I don't want to think about dying. I don't want to eat snakes either."

"Johnny could eat prickly pears," Frances said, "if he stays out here."

"He can't stay out here," Keith said. A sound came from him, as if he had snapped a twig.

"He could stay." Frances slid down onto her back. Something bright was happening to the mountains. I didn't know what it was, but it made me suddenly happy. I let her talk. I didn't have to be afraid of what she might say since we all seemed part of the same story, the Wild Child's story, and in his desert world everything seemed right. "We could be like the two sisters in a fairy tale," she went on, "who run away into the wild forest and live in their house among the animals. He could live among the coyotes and the jackrabbits."

"Fairy tales."

36

"Birds would talk to him in their own language, tell him where water is. Ants could help him build a house. He could live in the rain and the stars. He could make friends with the green Hell-Giants."

"Frances, what are you talking about?" Dennis asked. There was an odd sound in his voice, as if he badly wanted to know something she knew. "There are no Hell-Giants."

"Yes, there are. Their green fingers are all around you. They're down deep in the earth, where it's hot and fiery, and they want to come out where we are. But they can only get their thumbs and fingers out. They aren't evil, really, just too hot—"

"Are there really?" Dennis demanded.

Dan said dreamily, "Frances, you're cuckoo."

I thought she was, too, but I loved listening to her story.

"If they can get their fingers out, why can't they push the rest of themselves out?" Kelly asked. Frances thought awhile.

"Because their green toes are stuck in the other side of the world."

"Ster Thomas Augustine never said anything about Hell-Giants," Dennis said. But his voice wanted to believe in them. "She only said there was the devil. And saints. And God."

"And green Hell-Giants."

We were quiet again. I heard someone's stomach growl. The silver on the mountains turned bright, so bright I almost couldn't breathe. Then something huge and starry white began to lift itself into the sky. I could see faces again and a silver frost on the giants' fingers.

"The moon," Lupe whispered. Her earlobes trembled

with light. Dennis's red hair was frosted; his mouth was open. The moon was like an eye opening slowly above the black line of mountains. As it saw things, we could see them again, too.

"It's God," Lupe said reverently. I turned a little, to put my cheek against the ground. It was old; so was the moon. Saints, long division, the earth, fairy tales were all older than I could imagine. Even the words I spoke were older than I was. But in the night, under the still moonlight, I began to feel part of the oldness.

"There's a man in the moon," Dennis said.

"It's the Wild Child," I said.

"A cow jumped over the moon," Kelly murmured. "Then the fork ran away with the spoon."

Keith moved suddenly.

"Sh."

We froze. But whatever he heard was silent, and our eyes could not pick out the Wild Child among the cactuses. Keith sighed softly.

"Look at those stars." His voice was no longer angry. As the moon grew less bright, moving away from the mountains, the stars blazed from one end of the black sky to the other.

"That's where the Hell-Giants came from," Frances whispered. "That's what their fingers are reaching for. . . ." Then I saw one star apart from the great, blurred, brilliant mass of them, and I knew it was bigger than the world, bigger than the sun, older than I could imagine, and farther than any Hell-Giant could reach. My mind stopped reaching at the star across a vast, dark, terrifying nothing, and I

38

made the night sky flat again, with bright sand grains of stars, like a desert.

"Star light, star bright, first star I see tonight," Dennis murmured.

Keith rolled over, his face on one crooked arm. I heard his voice sigh again, softly. After a long time he said, "Frances . . . I don't think he'll come home. Not this time."

'I looked toward him. His voice sounded soft, twisted. Frances's voice came out of the night shadows.

"It's all right. The Hell-Giants will take care of him."

He called then, again and again, until his voice was gone. But no one came to him out of the darkness. We waited for a long time, until the night winds rose softly, whispered in the yucca leaves. The moon was in the middle of the sky, ringed with stars. It was darker, cooler, and all our stomachs were rumbling. Lupe stood up finally, brushed the dust off her skirt.

"I'd better go home," she said, "and help put the kids to bed."

"My dad's going to yell at me," Dennis commented, but he was still safe in the desert and not worried yet.

"That's nothing," Kelly said. "Wait till you hear our dad."

Keith got up finally, without saying anything, and we began to walk. We didn't get lost, or bump into a cactus, or step on scorpions; we just walked, as if we were all in the same dream and nothing could hurt us. Finally, we saw the church steeple and the lights from our neighborhood. Lupe's house was first. As she stepped in the front door, a flood of high-pitched Spanish came at her, faster than I thought anyone could talk. A baby started wailing, and she shut the door. We passed Dennis's house. He stopped in front of it, stood without moving until he swallowed. Then he went slowly into the yard. As he opened the door, it was wrenched away from him. He jerked back, away from a hand, but it reached out, following him, and smacked across his face. He started crying and talking at the same time. Dan whispered, "Jesus."

He and Kelly crossed the street to their house, walking close to each other. Keith came with Frances and me, stood with us beside the little peach tree in our front yard. He didn't say anything; he faced the desert again, where the winds were blowing from. Beyond it I could see lights. Our desert was only a tiny patch of darkness surrounded by the city. But the Wild Child had disappeared in it.

"Where is he?" Keith whispered. "Frances, where is he?"

I saw something out of the corner of my eye. Frances pointed, and he looked up to where a shooting star scarred the sky with gold and disappeared. He watched the sky long after it had gone. Then his head bowed. He put his hand on me lightly, and for a moment I listened to his breathing, smelled the sweat from his running. Then he jammed his hands into his pockets and walked into the night, while Frances and I went together back to the house.

2 ～ WILD BOARS

Three years later, we left the sunlit Arizona desert, crossed the sea, and moved into a tiny village in Germany. Instead of cactuses, jackrabbits, hot, wild winds, there was a ring of mountains jutting up into the sky and a cold green river that went from one secret place to another, chattering to itself as it passed by the village in a language I didn't understand.

I had grown in three years. So had Frances. She had gotten most of her teeth back, and she wore glasses, so she could see pine needles instead of a cloudy blur when she looked at a tree. Her nose was too big; her eyes were too round; her short hair went flying in all directions. Nothing she wore fit her right. I kept waiting for all the different parts of her to start to match. But neither of us had much hope in it.

I opened the door to our new house at twilight the first evening we were there and went outside. I had to go alone because I couldn't find Frances. I listened for kids' voices shouting through a soft, vast desert evening, but I heard only a cow moo from the pasture behind the house. I smelled manure, river water, something dark and chilly that was the night seeping down through the mountains. I went down the drive, crossed the strip of cobbled road. I was picking my way over three sets of railroad tracks when a small man in a uniform came out of the station house and shouted at me. I had no idea what he was saying, so I ignored him and found my way to the river. A hill of trees too steep to climb rose sharply from the opposite bank, flung a dark reflection across the water. I found a dry stone at the riverbank and sat down.

I had read a little about Germany before we moved. It was a country in Europe; it had been badly bombed during World War II and was still trying to recover. I hoped no one would start World War III while I was there. I didn't see any evidence of war. There were just a hundred people living along a mountain road, growing cows and vegetables, and collecting smelly piles of hay and cowshit beside their front doors. They spoke a strange, harsh language; they made sausages that were three feet long and big, dark wheels of hot bread. My father already bought some from behind one of the secret doors beside the road.

I settled a little deeper into the rock. There were no Hell-Giants in that country, only trees, tall and dark with twilight. There was, I realized slowly, nowhere to go. No play-ground to run to in the evening, no desert to hide in, no houses whose doors would open to me, no friends. There was one road and a hundred million trees.

I stared at my dark shadow in the water, longing for home, too miserable to cry. A train roared into the station, full of strangers going to unfamiliar places. Bells rang, lights flashed at the station house, until the train whistled and snaked away into the night. Some animal bellowed into the silence. I heard a door open; a woman called a name. I knew it was a name because her voice was pitched to an uncertain distance, and the word was broken into two sad notes.

"Brot," I said to the river. "Butter, eins, zwei, drei." Then I echoed the woman softly. "Hel-mut. Hel-mut."

"Ja?" someone answered questioningly. The back hairs on my neck prickled, for the word seemed to come from a tree. Then one of the trees moved, turned into a boy walk-ing down the riverbank toward me. I couldn't see his face well; his hair was light, and he wore funny thick leather shorts. His legs were bare; his shoes were big and clumsy. He squatted down on the bank next to me. He regarded me steadily a moment. Then he said, "One, two, three, four, five. Good morning, good evening, my name is Helmut."

"Guten Abend," I said carefully.

"Wie heissen Sie?"

"Huh?" Then the words made sense in my mind, and I told him.

"Sprechen Sie deutsch?"

"No. Nein." My father's German lessons had been very basic. I added, not to be totally outdone, "Guten Morgen.

Kirche. Schule. Badezimmer. Sechs, sieben, acht, neun, zehn."

He nodded gravely. "You are *Amerikanerin*. I speak English in *Schule*. Why are you sitting here?"

I shrugged. "There's nothing else to do. Where do you live?"

"Beside you." He pointed to a light at one side of our house and said something unintelligible. He translated slowly. "My mother built your house. It is new."

"I know." It was a pretty house, with polished wood floors and walls, a staircase, two balconies, and a beautiful tile stove in the living room for heat.

"She has chickens."

"Who?"

"My mother. And a cow."

"Oh." I added politely, "That's nice."

"My uncle owns *das Gasthaus*."

"*Das* what?"

He searched for a word, gave up. "Where people sleep, off the trains, or when they fish. Also, there is beer. And *Schnecken*. I find *Schnecken* for him in a bucket when it is raining."

"*Schnecken*." I couldn't imagine anything in America that you put in a bucket while it rained. "Worms? For fishing?"

"*Ach*, no." He smiled again, groping lightly in the air with his fingers for the word, as if he were reaching for a moth. But it eluded him in the dusk. "They have tiny houses. They carry them on their backs."

For a moment something in me seemed to wake up,

blinking curiously at the strange world. Then I said, "Snails."

"*Ja*. Snails. Big, fat white snails—they are good to eat here."

I swallowed a tasteless lump in my throat. "Raw?"

"*Bitte?*"

"Do you cook them?"

"Ah. *Ja. Mit Butter*. And—" His fingers grasped again at night wings. "It is *weiss*. White. Like a bulb. It smells sharp."

I shook my head dumbly, and he gave up on that one. The woman's voice came again across the evening. "Helmut."

"*Ach*." His body unfolded a little; then he settled down again. "You are *schöne*. Pretty."

I stared at him. "Thanks," I said after a moment. "*Danke*."

He smiled. Then he leaned forward swiftly and kissed my cheek. "You *mein* girlfriend. *Ja?* Yes." He nodded for both of us. "Okay."

I watched him jog through the trees, across the tracks. I stood up suddenly, shouting, "Garlic! It's garlic!"

I found Frances when I got back home, needing her to talk to. "I have a boyfriend," I said, amazed. I sprawled across a fat, soft bed, picking at the quilt. "He wears weird leather shorts, and he eats snails." My fingers found and drew out a little white feather from the quilt. "Feathers. Millions and millions of feathers. No wonder it's so soft."

There was something in the back of her mind she was afraid of. I knew it, and I didn't want to think about it, but finally, I let her say it.

"We have to go to school tomorrow."

I was silent a moment, thinking of desks, rules, a roomful of unpredictable voices. "Maybe it won't be so bad." But I didn't believe it.

"It's always bad. I hate school. I hate it so much."

"You'll be all right. It's a school on the base; there won't be any nuns."

"That won't make any difference," she said glumly. Then she pushed up her glasses with one finger and reached for a book. But she didn't read. I was silent, feeling her dread the morning.

We woke up in darkness, got dressed in a chilly house, ate thick hot toast and butter. Everything smelled strange: the new house, the battered air force bus that picked us up, the fields growing pale with dawn. The day was a bland blur of new faces, waxed green floors, soggy spinach and peanut-butter sandwiches, new books, chalk, drawing paper, the smell of paste. Naturally we had to get up and tell the class what our names were and where we were from. Every face in the room had a different history. We had been collected at random from one end of a continent to the other and thrown together into sixth grade in a foreign country by the vague mysterious workings of the government. Most of the class lived in apartments on the base. There were only a few of us bussed out of the tiny island of Amerika back into the German countryside. The bus ride back home through the mountains was beautiful, and I tried to cheer Frances up with that. But she only stared at a little roadside shrine, built for somebody who had driven over the cliff, and didn't answer.

I saw Helmut as we took the last steep curve down into the village. He was walking along the road with a satchel slung over his shoulder. I waved at him. His face broke into a grin, and he waved back, loping after the bus.

By daylight his skin was pink and white. His hair was straw-colored, and his eyes were a very dark blue. He was slender, sturdy, and cheerful. He waited for me on the lawn while I changed clothes. By the time I came down he was surrounded by curious village kids. They chanted, "One, two, three, four, five," at me until Helmut told them to *"raus!"* They scattered and lighted again nearby like a flock of birds.

"They live there," he said, nodding at a big, teetering house on the other side of us. The front yard was a big vegetable garden.

"All of them?" There seemed a dozen of them, all skinny, with runny noses and tangled, chattery voices.

"Their father owns the cows behind your house." He paused, proud of the sentence, and I laughed. He grinned amiably and put his arm around my shoulders. He smelled of sweat, fresh air, leather. He had nice cheekbones. "You laugh at me." Then he turned. People had come up behind us. "This is Heidi. This is Wilhelm."

Heidi was plump, braided and pretty as a doll. She smiled at me and said, *"Guten Tag,"* in a shy, grave voice. Then she said something else that Helmut translated carefully.

"Your father buys her mother's *Brot*—bread!"

"Sehr gut," Wilhelm said critically. Wilhelm was old and dignified, at least sixteen, and his English was far better than Helmut's. He said to me, "Will your father be

at home? I would like to speak English with him, to learn about America."

I nodded, suddenly shy under the intense gaze of his glasses. "He'll be home this evening. You can ask him then."

"Wilhelm goes with the train to Trier to the *Gymnasium*," Helmut said. "His father owns that." He pointed to the train station, where the little man had come out like a cuckoo-clock figure to shout at me the first night. Helmut let go of me.

"I must go to my uncle." His kiss landed on my jaw; he ran down the road toward the *Gasthaus*. I watched his bare legs move, long and effortless in their clunky shoes. Then I wandered down to the river. I found the little kids there already, on the bank, peeing in the shallow part of the river, giggling and flicking water at each other. I leaned against a tree, watching. A strong, dark wave of homesickness rolled through me suddenly. I wanted the desert. I wanted a hamburger. I wanted Lupe Ramirez and Keith and games of tag and hide-and-seek in the twilight. There were cows here, but no bicycles. Nobody knew me. I couldn't read their books. Everything was worn, slightly dirty, and old, even the river. There was no ice-cream truck, no television, no Hershey bars. Just cobblestones, piles of hay and cowshit, and strange faces. I pushed myself away from the tree after a while and collapsed in misery on the porch step in front of our house. After a while Frances joined me, so I could talk.

"I want to go home." I tilted my head back and shouted, "I want to go home!" Nobody answered except chickens

48

making stupid noises in the next yard. "There's no place to go at night."

"Sh," Frances said. So I shut up. We gazed across the river at the darkening pine. I could hear the river's voice through the still air, telling a story without an end. I listened harder, trying to separate one word from another. After a while I heard Frances's voice, soft and faraway, dreaming aloud.

"So the two sisters lived together in one house. One was very beautiful and smart—"

"Clever."

"Clever. The other was ugly, and she never learned to talk. Sometimes they fought, and sometimes they loved each other. The beautiful one had gold hair to her ankles and blue eyes, and she wore a crown of roses that never died. The ugly one was little and dark, with a big nose. She had a pet bird, though, that always sat on her wrist . . . the most beautiful red bird in the world. It talked for her. And they lived in the deep forest, by a river with secret trees all around them. And inside the trees lived secret things."

"What kinds of things?"

"Secrets. Little, tangled, twisted things you find in trees, with lots of fingers and their eyes in the wrong places . . . They whispered and whispered at night, but they never harmed the two sisters. Until one day—"

"Frances! Oh, there you are. Come and eat."

The river had swallowed the voices of the children. Twilight was misting between the trees. My mother's voice hung like a good sound in the air, like a part of a different story, one without confusions, bewilderments, secret faces.

49

I wanted to hug her suddenly, so I did. She ruffled my hair.

"You're getting taller."

"I am?"

"Soon you'll turn into a pretty lady and go away and leave me."

"No, I won't." I thought of pictures in magazines, of women wearing stockings, red lipstick, not a hair out of place, who put all the stories neatly away at night and never dreamed. "Not ever. I'm not going to leave you."

"You'll want to."

"No, I won't. Ever."

The days began to make a pattern of books and desks, homework, Helmut, and a twilight full of smells and river stories, five days a week. On Saturday my father drove us to catechism and confession on the base. We were going through questions in the Baltimore Catechism for the third time. I wondered what marvels of divinity we would be ready to understand if we ever reached the end of it. When we came home, a lunch of chewy, fresh *Brötchen,* tangy Germany sausage and cheese made up for the rigors of theology and the shadowy humiliations of the confessional. Saturdays brought out unholy things in Frances.

"I can't stand confession," she said wildly one morning, while she was searching under the bed for her slip. "I can't stand it, I can't stand it—"

"What's so hard about it?"

"I don't know how to tell the truth. I don't know how to say what my mind is thinking. I can't help seeing all the secret things in the trees—"

"What?"

"And that big black horse on the way to school, and the

50

two ducks the other day—and that white cloth Christ is always wearing when they take off all His other clothes—"

"Frances!"

"I can't help it!" She couldn't find her slip; she sat down disconsolately on the bed in her underpants and socks. Then she looked down at herself. She pinched her chest. "I'm growing."

"You are not. You're flat as a pancake."

"I am, too."

"Hurry up!"

"Look at that."

"Frances! Will you get dressed! You want to go to confession naked?"

"No." She sighed and slid off the bed. "I just wish my mind would be quiet. I wish I could stop thinking. I wish I were a red bird and I could fly away. I wish, I wish, I wish . . ."

The next day she wished me into her story. I went with Helmut and Wilhelm on a long hike into the hills. It was early spring. We followed an underground stream on a gentle slope upward into the forests. The pine trees were growing new fingers of pale green. They gave off a sweet, dusky smell of pitch and bark and old dry needles. Wilhelm and Helmut veered between English and German, discussing some grave matter. I was too busy to listen; Helmut drifted to my side now and then to tell me the German names for wild flowers. I watched him spring lightly from rock to stump in his heavy shoes. Then I watched a red bird fly between the pine boughs. I stooped to smell violets growing in the dark, moist twists of roots. The underground stream danced to the surface, sparkled over a tangle of branches; I cupped cold water in my hands and drank it. Ferns were uncurling around it. The ground I stood on was soft and dark; I left my footprints in it. I found red speckled mushrooms beside a mossy log, and I stooped again, hugging my knees, staring at them. The forest held out a different secret every time I looked at it: a new color, a shape of rock, a shift of light. It crowded into my eyes. I was walking in a timeless forest, where children left trails of breadcrumbs and followed talking birds. The stones were still only when I looked at them. The water flowed out of vast, dark places beneath the mountain. The trees' hands moved in the wind, beckoning toward the distance where tree faces melted into each other, and light and shadow blurred into a mystery.

Something white lay beneath a fern: another color, a different secret. I picked it up as I rose. Black, empty eyes stared at me across a broad band of bone. It narrowed into a snout. Two tusks curved against my wrist. I dropped it, yelling. One rotten tusk thumped to the ground at my feet, but Helmut caught the skull as it fell.

"Boar," Wilhelm said. He glanced around curiously. The silence thundered suddenly with the imminence of boars. "If you go too far into the mountains, you might see them. They are dangerous."

"I'm not going out there again," I told Frances after I got home safely. "Ever."

"You went into the desert, where there were rattlesnakes."

"That's different. You just stand very still when you hear a rattlesnake. But boars! They have little pig eyes and bristles, and they grunt and rip you in two with their whit tusks. And they're all around us. In the secret mountains all around us."

She didn't answer, and I knew why. Her mind was busy again, spinning boars into her forests.

So I didn't go far from the village after that. I helped Helmut collect snails on damp afternoons. I bought penny candy from his uncle in the *Gasthaus,* where the air smelled of hard toffee, polished wood, tobacco, and beer. I helped chase cows out of the backyard when they broke through the fence. I watched a tempest rage across the steep hill behind the river, bending trees until they moaned, and I hugged the tile stove to warm my bones again, thinking of boars.

Spring bloomed across the mountains. Buttercups came up everywhere overnight. I couldn't stop touching the rich, moist gold of their petals. Roses in our front yard burst into fiery colors; I buried my face in them, smelling them, wanting to eat them. Helmut's mother's cow started to look as if she had swallowed a garbage can. She had a calf; the little meadow where we took them to pasture was speckled with wild flowers. The air was full of spiders' castings, hair-fine glintings that vanished when I tried to see them. I wanted to run into the brightness, away from God, sixth grade, peanut-butter sandwiches, and Frances's anxious, questioning face. But I couldn't run. In the mountains, with the shadows from rain clouds streaking down their flanks, the pine trees bristling toward the sky, the boars were rousing.

Helmut was suddenly afflicted with an odd uneasiness. He grew listless, his bucket clanking emptily against his knee while he let snail after snail creep away from under his nose. He forgot how to speak English. One Sunday, when we sat on the porch watching the grownups parade gravely up and down the road in their best black clothes, I asked him what was wrong. He looked at me blankly. I tried it in German.

"*Was ist los?*"

His body fidgeted; he muttered something in German.

"Let's go for a walk down the tracks," I suggested.

"*Nein.*"

"Let's go look at the tadpoles." There were thousands of them in a little bog by the river, being slowly eaten by their parents.

"*Bitte?*" he said absently. He was frowning at some invisible point in front of him, between him and the adults strolling placidly back and forth.

"Look at that," I said. "There's Heidi's parents. There's Wilhelm's father. There's your mother with your uncle. They see each other every day. Your mother trades eggs for Heidi's mother's bread. But on Sundays, they're so polite, not even laughing, as if they're strangers just meeting."

He made another absent noise. He shifted to drape his arms on his bare knees and rest his chin on them. His frown had deepened. "What's the matter?" I asked again. But his body only jerked a little at my voice, and he didn't answer.

He came over with Wilhelm again after supper, but instead of lounging with me on the lawn, he trailed Wilhelm into the house to talk to my father. I was angry. I sat on the steps with my chin in my fists, watching the little *Kinder* playing in the street. I was never sure how many of them lived next door; their numbers changed constantly.

54

They were as noisy as ever. The little girls were barefoot, and the two-year-old's diaper was falling off. They waved at me to come and play, but I shook my head. Presently they drifted down the road into the twilight. I stopped being angry and began to wonder what ailed Helmut. My mind puzzled bits and pieces of him into a picture. Blue eyes. Pale, curly hair. Big, rough hands, brisk at picking up snails or leading his mother's calf home, slow, almost dreamy at other things. A sweaty, grassy smell. A quick, happy laugh that I hadn't heard recently. Long, sturdy legs from hiking up the mountain to school in the next village. There was a fine dust of hair on them. I watched his legs idly, leaping the stream in the little pasture, jogging the last half mile down the road into the village. I watched them move until suddenly I couldn't sit still any longer. I stood up, my mind full of flowers and boar skulls and a strange, terrible impatience.

I wanted to run; there was no place to run to. I wanted my bones to turn to thistledown, my face to change. I wanted the boars to come pounding through the village, silvery with wind, their hollow eyes like black fire, their tusks rooting up cobblestones, manure piles, railway tracks, clucking hens, the walls of the house where my father and Wilhelm and Helmut sat peacefully practicing English. "The boars are here," I wanted to shout as the dark, powerful bellowing poured into the house. "Here!" But no boars came. As I stood listening for them, only Helmut came, opening the door and closing it softly behind him.

He didn't see me. He stood two feet from me, staring down at the steps. His hands were clenched. His face looked stiff and strange. I wondered, astonished, if he were

55

about to cry. I saw him swallow. Then he whispered one word, very softly.

He walked past me. As if the unfamiliar word had put a spell on me, I couldn't move or speak. At the end of the drive he stopped again. His hands opened; he turned his head almost hesitantly to look back.

I went to him, walked with him across the tracks to the riverbank. We sat down on the rocks, watched the water darken. He said nothing for a long time, until his body made a sudden movement, half twisting, half shuddering, and he said to the water, his voice high, pleading, like a child's, *"Ich verstehe nicht. . . ."* The dark trees seemed to lean inward to hear his words. When we went home, he didn't speak or touch me, as if I were only a shadow in the dusk.

He grew increasingly moody as the days passed. He wouldn't talk to me; he wouldn't come to the house to bring me an odd hen's egg, or show off what new English he had learned that day, or give me a bite of one of his mother's tortes, covered with unsweetened whipped cream and grape halves.

"What's eating him?" I demanded of Frances. "What did I do wrong?"

But she couldn't help me, and I was growing half-afraid of her. She had never known how to exist very well among people, and she was getting worse instead of better. At school she would walk with her head ducked down, so that her hair hid her eyes. When anyone spoke to her, her body would twist uneasily away. She swallowed her voice; what she had left was barely more than a whisper. It was all the strange thoughts in her head that made her strange, I knew.

She was beginning to turn into someone I was afraid I might hate, but I didn't know how to make her stop thinking.

"You read too much." She carried stacks of library books home and lay on her bed reading for hours. I couldn't stop her, but I didn't think it was good for her. *"Andersen's Fairytales. The Borrowers. Sue Barton. Nancy Drew, Girl Detective. Mary Poppins. Adam of the Road. Ben and Me.* You read them all in three days. You look funny, with your glasses, carrying that big stack of books."

She turned a page and said, "Shut up."

"You fill up your mind with books like you're trying not to think of something."

Her eyes went wide behind her glasses. She stared at the pages in front of her a moment. Then she rolled off the bed, went downstairs. She went into the exact center of the lawn and lay down. She took off her glasses, tilted her head to stare at the sky. She frowned at it, blinking, a long time. Then she rolled over and spoke with her face in the grass.

"Until one day . . . the two sisters started to understand the whisperings. One of them—the ugly one—"

"No, the beautiful one."

"No, the ugly one—wanted to leave the house, follow all the whisperings to see where they led. But the beautiful one said that the forest was a terrible place, full of wicked things, skulls, and dead birds, boars and trees with roots like snakes that caught you but wouldn't let go. She said it was better to stay home, cooking and cleaning the house and feeding the deer. She was afraid her crown of roses would die, away from their forest house.

"But the ugly one kept listening to the whisperings, and

listening . . . she couldn't stop. There was something in the deep forest she wanted. The beautiful one said no, it was terrible, a horrible monster, sleeping in the dark. And the ugly sister knew the beautiful sister was right. But still, she kept listening, wanting. . . . Finally, one evening, she tossed the red bird free into the air and began to follow it. . . ."

Her voice faded. I lay very still. It was nearly summer. The blue, smoky air seemed timeless. Moths chased each other in pale, fluttery circles. I could hear the sound of a voice in the train station, a cow in the back pasture pulling grass, a door closing, as clearly as if they were all beside me. I got up and began to walk.

I found Helmut picking snails out of his mother's garden. They looked fat and healthy, fed on her vegetables, and they made squishy clinks hitting one another in the bucket. He didn't seem surprised to see me. He said tonelessly, *"Tag,"* and picked a snail off a green tomato. His knees were dirty, and there was a streak of dirt on his nose.

I stopped in front of him, until he had to look at me. Then I said softly, "What's wrong? Why don't you talk to me anymore?"

"Bitte?"

"You know what I'm saying. Stop pretending. Ever since you talked to my father and Wilhelm that night, you haven't talked to me. Why? What did they say to you?"

He didn't answer. His hands had lost their briskness. They moved with an underwater slowness, wrestling to separate a snail from the vine. His brows were pinched; he didn't look at me but at the snails, which seemed stronger than his fingers. He shook his head finally. *"Nein."*

"*Nein,* what?"

"Ask your father. Ask Wilhelm."

"I'm asking you!"

He said something sharply, glaring at me. Then he realized that it was useless insulting me in German. He turned away from me. His hands snapped out in all directions, and snails somersaulted into the bucket. It was half-full, and the sky was darkening. I knew he would stop soon. I gazed at his back, puzzled. Then I said, "What is it? Don't you like me anymore? What does *Juden* mean?"

His shoulders jumped. He said again, *"Nein,"* but his voice was very soft. His hands dropped to his sides, then downward to touch the dark, lumpy ground. I took a step forward, bewildered and troubled.

"Helmut."

He straightened, turning finally. There was a feeling in him I recognized. His body made little, unfinished movements; his eyes swept the twilight, searching for a place to run to. But there was no place, only the mountains ringing us. His face was pale, tense with words he would not say. He reached for the bucket finally, swung out of the garden toward the *Gasthaus.*

I had to hurry to keep up with him. I was angry and hurt, but I didn't want to leave him, I wanted to understand him. He said one incomprehensible thing finally. "It's why your father is here. The war."

"World War III?" I said, alarmed. But he only took a snail out of the bucket and threw it as hard as he could against the station house. He wouldn't answer any of my questions. He kicked open the gate to the *Gasthaus* and

59

went to the front, where his uncle, in his leather beer-serving apron, was smoking a pipe.

His uncle looked surprised, and so was I, because Helmut always took the snails around the back to the kitchen. His uncle, a big gray-haired man with a great mustache, made what sounded like a mild protest. Helmut stopped short on the walk. His face seemed frozen suddenly. He gazed at his uncle as if they were strangers, with the twilight between them. He drew breath suddenly, his face drained white, to ask a question. But somehow his uncle, standing so placidly, well fed, and prosperous in the tranquil German evening, answered it before he asked. He turned the bucket of snails upside down and threw it on the walk. The snails spilled out, and he began smashing them methodically under his heavy shoes.

I was appalled. His uncle's pipe fell out of his mouth. He seemed too astonished to be angry. *"Was machst du?"* he breathed. Then he closed a big hand at the nape of Helmut's neck and shook him. Helmut was crying. The blood swelled into his uncle's face then, as he stared at the pale, sticky mess of snails. Helmut broke away before his uncle began to bellow. He ran toward the gate; his uncle, pursuing, splintered more snails underfoot. I watched one snail that had escaped the slaughter grope blindly over the pieces of the dead. Then I ran, gasping and sobbing, back to the house. I pounded upstairs and rolled into a ball on my bed, surrounded by all of Frances's books.

Helmut was possessed by a devil, I decided, when I had finished crying. I thought of asking my father what he and Wilhelm had said to make Helmut so angry with the world. But my father's mind seemed too gentle to understand Hel-

mut's boot crushing down onto the defenseless heads and
houses of snails. It was a devil made for children.

I found Helmut after school the next day, raking out a
stable for a neighbor, who lived for some reason above his
cows. I didn't know what to say, so I walked past quickly,
on my way to buy bread. But Helmut called to me hesitantly. I stopped.

We looked at each other over the cowshit he was piling up.

"Why did—why did you do that?" I whispered.

But he only looked away from me, down to the muck at
his feet. He said, "Heinz is picking snails now. The *Kinder*
help him. It is okay."

"But why?" My voice still wouldn't come. He wouldn't
answer. The cows were bellowing in the fields, and he
began raking again.

But as I turned, he added, "Later. You will walk with me?
Yes? Okay?"

"Okay."

He would splash along the river with me or practice his
English homework with me, but he wouldn't talk. It was
not only to me, I discovered, but to my parents, his mother,
anyone. He had no more attacks of insanity, but he hid a
secret inside him, as stubbornly as Frances hid her secret
imaginings from everyone but me. They both were possessed, with devils who raged silently, like the boars within
the deep forests, but who could not speak.

Summer came finally, and another year of school ended.
The mountains turned fiery; the air stank of fertilizer. It
seemed to crackle silently, waiting for a storm. My parents
took us away from the village for a week, to visit ancient

churches, castles, ruins. I came back with my head dizzy with strange names: Köln, Oberammergau, Neuschwanstein, Bacharach, München. I tried to tell Helmut what I had seen: "A coach of real gold that a king rode in. The true robe of Christ, with the outline of His body on it. Castles hundreds of years old, on the edge of a beautiful river. A big clock tower, with figures that come out playing musical instruments every hour. A restaurant with huge barrels of beer, where even nuns eat, and they take pictures of you."

But he only grunted, rattling his rake over the cobblestones. "My uncle would like the beer hall," he said.

He had shrunk into himself, snaillike, and he wouldn't come out. I missed him, but I pretended not to. I turned to Frances, who was garnering treasures out of her constant reading, out of the landscape, forcing me to listen to her. More and more often at twilight she would go down to the river, let her mind drift into the current, flow deeper and deeper into the forests, and soon her voice would whisper out of the water, *Once upon a time* . . . She would put gold into her stories, and old stone towers, kings and queens in palaces with enormous gardens. But when I asked her where the red bird went, she only said, "It's dangerous."

Finally, deep in midsummer, everything ended. I came to the stables one morning, while Helmut was cleaning them, and balanced myself on the gate. I felt peculiar words in me. Helmut was raking a stall; he didn't notice me until he turned to toss the pile out of the gate. He straightened, surprised that I hadn't spoken. I looked at him a moment; then I said the strange words.

"We're moving to England."

His head gave a little shake. I saw him swallow. "No. You are staying here three years."

"They don't need my father here anymore. They're sending him to England."

He rested the rake gently against the side of the stall and climbed the other side of the gate. "No," he pleaded. I pushed my glasses up my nose, not wanting to cry.

"I can't help it. Anyway, I want to go."

"No."

"They speak English there. They don't eat snails. You never talk to me anyway."

His hands twisted on the gate. "You do not understand—"

"You don't give me a chance. I can't even tell if you like me or not."

I paused. Things had happened to him without my noticing. The light tan on his face made his eyes very blue; the hot summer sun had beaten down into his hair. As I stared at him, his hands rose suddenly, as if to cover his face. Then he touched my wrist. "Don't go. You don't—you don't understand."

"You won't let me!" I shouted. He jerked a little, the gate rattling in his hold. "I don't know why you're so angry with the world. I don't know why you smashed all those snails. I'm sick of being in a mountain prison. Everywhere I look, there they are, full of skulls. I don't understand anything. I'm tired of my face."

"Wait—" Then his face froze, and he couldn't speak. He turned away, picked up the rake. "*Ach,*" he said miserably. "Go to England. I don't care."

I slid down off the gate. It was an idiotic country anyway,

full of ruined castles and snails. They couldn't even make a french fry right. I kicked at stones along the roadside, my throat burning. I didn't care either. I would go to distant places, and he could stay here forever, raking stables. I went home, slouched around the house all day, reading, knowing exactly when he was walking to school, when he would be coming home. I found myself daydreaming by a window, so I yelled at Frances awhile. "Look at you! Daydreaming, while he's growing taller and turning into gold. You're getting fat, and not even in the right places. You're ugly, ugly, with your freckles and your glasses. You don't even have any bones in your face. Look at you in the window. Look!" But she wouldn't look. She just drew her knees up and hid her face against them. The morning burned into noon, into a sweaty, airless afternoon that buzzed with insects. I went down to the river, stared at the water, wondering where it went. A train boomed by, following the water. Where did it go? Germany? France? Austria? Poland? I was surrounded by mysteries, places of war. But that had happened before I was born. And nothing had happened for a thousand years to this small village.

A sound began tearing into my thoughts. At first I thought it was an insect or a distant train whistle. Then it came clearer, a high, constant, anguished screaming that made my heart pound. I ran up the bank, across the tracks. The train seemed to have sucked all sound, all motion with it. The only sound in the village was the screaming; nothing else seemed to be alive.

For a moment it was a nightmare: the hot, dusty, empty houses; the frantic, disembodied screaming. My mouth went dry; my throat made a convulsive whimper. Then a door swung open; the neighbor children streamed out of their house, in front of their mother, who held a baby in her arms. Its terrible crying made my knees weak. But their mother called to me, and I ran across the street to her.

"*Bitte—*" she gasped. "*Bitte—*" The rest of what she said was incomprehensible. I stared down at the baby. It was tiny, dark-haired. Pushing under its skull, down into its brain, was a big purplish tumor, and it could not get away from the pain.

I caught a word finally and said numbly, "My father is at work." My mother came running out of the house then. She took the baby, made soothing noises at the mother, but I could tell she didn't understand the tumult of words. I saw Helmut then, jogging down into the village, and I shouted at him so hard my voice cracked.

He joined us, the color blanching out of his face when he saw the baby. "She must to go to the doctor in Trier," he said to my mother.

But my father had the car, and he wouldn't be home for two hours. "Why didn't she go before?" I whispered. "Look at it." I saw my mother's face. "It's going to die."

"They are so poor," Helmut said softly. "So many *Kinder.*" They were surrounding us, barefoot, dirty-faced, frightened at the baby's torment. We weren't rich, but at least, when I was sick, I went to a doctor. I realized then something of what poverty was. Helmut added a few words in German to the woman. Then he turned and ran toward the *Gasthaus.* The woman, her fingers at her eyes, her mouth, watched him. My mother tried to quiet the baby, but it was rigid with pain. The children stood like statues in the hot dust. They ate bread and butter and sugar to keep their stomachs quiet. Their teeth were going bad before they even lost them.

There was the roar of an engine down the street. A battered truck jerked toward us, with Helmut on the running board. It coughed to a stop near us. Helmut's uncle got down, opened the passenger door, talking and patting the woman's shoulder. He took the baby from my mother, gave it to Helmut. Helmut's face lifted sharply, the skin pulling across his bones. Then he drew air and touched the hot red face, murmuring. He started to get into the truck beside the woman. But she stopped him and stretched her hand toward my mother.

"Please," she begged, and my mother took the baby and climbed up into the truck beside her. It shook nervously, then rattled away down the road, following the train tracks. Helmut watched it.

"The truck is dying," he said. His voice shook. *"Mein Gott,* such a tiny child. No one is keeping the *Gasthaus;* he left it by itself for the baby."

He started walking. I thought he was going to the *Gasthaus,* but he walked past it out of the village. I had to work to keep up with him. Neither of us spoke. I didn't care where he was going. I wanted to go far, as far away as possible from the frightened children and the baby with the terrible death pushing into its mind. Helmut followed the river a ways, clambering over rocks, skirting brambles and stinging nettles. Then he turned upward toward the mountains and began to climb.

We climbed high, higher than I had ever been before. Sometimes the slope was so steep I slipped on loose needles and had to stop to keep the pain from boring into my side.

66

I could hear Helmut's sturdy breathing after a while, but he never stopped. The trees standing straight against the slopes whispered in the wind. Light and shadows shifted under my hands as I groped at granite to keep my balance. Sometimes the slope leveled and we walked in deep forest, hidden in shadow, where tiny things grew in secret. Sometimes we trudged upward against the warm, roaring wind. It was pushing bulky clouds white as tusks over the top of the mountain to peer down at us.

Finally, we reached the open face of the slope, our feet deep in dry golden grass. A pile of granite thrust out of the high point of the clearing; above it was dark forest. Helmut edged toward the boulders. From the other side of them I heard water. He reached them finally, but instead of resting in their shadow, he climbed onto the biggest one and stood looking down over the valley.

I climbed up beside him, not standing but hugging the rock, and peeked over the edge. I felt my heart fall through nothingness, and I shut my eyes, trying to push myself into the boulder. After a while I opened my eyes again, and then my fear fell away.

The river wove a green and silver thread through the valley, as far as I could see. Our village was a tiny, ancient thing, grown out of the land, belonging to the mountains. The mountains surrounded it, their faces beautiful and harsh, with sunny green slopes, crumbling peaks of stone, dark woods. Beyond them lay the misty blue of other mountains. Beside us, a clear stream slid over a cut in the rocks and fell ten feet into nothingness, fanning into a delicate, sunlit spray before the earth caught it again.

I stopped clinging so hard to the rock. The world seemed

to spread out before us like an untold tale. I felt strange so high above it, as if I had disappeared. I could almost see Frances, a short, stubby-haired, anxious girl with glasses, down beside the river, whispering stories to herself. Then Helmut pitched a piece of stone down into nothingness. I watched it bounce off the cliff and into trees below, and I gripped the rock again.

He began to talk. Sometimes his voice was soft, precise, the words sounding dry and scratchy out of his throat. At other times his voice would grow husky with tears, and he would wipe them angrily out of his eyes. Sometimes his fists would pound soundlessly down on the rock, and his language would be harsh, ugly, as if he were mocking it unconsciously. It took me a long time to piece together what he must have been saying and feeling because he spoke almost entirely in German.

As it was, I got a glimpse of some enormity within the secret places of the beautiful land. There were boar skulls everywhere, in unexpected places, with their black, hollow eyes and murderous tusks. "Millions," he said once. "Millions of people. They put them in ovens to die." He veered into English again later. "I am afraid of my mother, my uncle. I am afraid to know. What they did. What they knew. I do not want to know." After a long time, his voice grown empty, weary, he whispered, "I cannot go away from it. This is my home."

He was silent at last, his head bowed. Even his hands were quiet. I was lying on my back, with my arm over my eyes. I felt cold and sick. I didn't understand what he had told me; I knew only that he was right: There was no place to go, not even into the soft blue faraway mountains, to get away from the world.

I heard him shift. Then I felt his fingers, lifting my wrist away from my eyes. His face looked tired, pale. "You can go away from it," he said, "To England. They hate us there." The late sunlight was hitting his face. His lashes were the same pale gold as his hair. His eyes were troubled, vivid in the light. I could feel my heart thumping suddenly in my throat. My hands wanted to do things they had never done before: touch his hair, his hurt face, his shoulder. I didn't know if he would let me. I didn't know how the expression in his eyes would change if I lifted my hand away from the rock and touched the triangle of sun on his cheek. Then his own hand moved again. I felt him touch my hair, and I stopped breathing. He blinked a little, as if surprised at something in himself. Then he leaned over me, shadowing my face. His lips parted a little; I could hear his breathing. Slowly, carefully, almost hesitantly, he began smoothing my hair back from my face, while I lay so still I thought I must have turned to glass, and all the winds in the world had vanished.

Then a hoarse, snorting bellow broke out of the mountains around us. The wind pounced down at me as I shrieked. I sat up; Helmut cried at me, startled. I slid off the rock so fast I fell and banged my knee. He called me again, but I was already running, straight down the slope, as fast as I could without breaking my neck, while the boars roared out of the trees around me, with silver bristles and great tusks and terrible, empty eyes.

They pursued me all the way down the mountain. Sometimes I fell, and I heard their crackling behind me. I heard Helmut calling me, but I couldn't stop. After a while I heard nothing but my own breath, tearing at my throat. I was whimpering when I finally reached the bottom. I had run out of the sunlight into dusk; the ground was cool when I collapsed on it.

I hugged the ground, crying until I got my breath back. My teeth hurt; my ribs hurt; my lungs felt scraped raw. I heard Helmut talking hoarsely at me in German as he paced circles around me. He stopped talking finally and dropped down beside me, panting. I began to hear the river again. A cow mooed in the distance. The world was making familiar noises.

I rolled over, saw Helmut upside down. I sat up, and the mountains toppled back into place. Helmut's face was flushed, sweating. He was staring at me incredulously.

"You ran down the mountain. Stupid. *Dummkopf*. Idiot. You could have killed yourself. Why do you run? Did you— did you run away from me?"

I shook my head. My throat still ached with fear and exhaustion. "No. It was the boars."

His eyes were miserable again, hurt. "You never have to run from me."

"No," I said again. "The boars."

"What boars?"

"I heard them. You heard them—"

"No—"

"They were coming out of the trees, they would have killed us—"

His voice rose. "What boars?"

I stared at him. He slid his hands up over his face wearily, murmuring, "Boars. There were no boars. Only us."

"But the noise—"

"There was no noise. Only water. Only wind." He slumped over himself, sifting road dust in one hand. He whispered after a long time, "No. You ran from me."

He got up, began to walk again, his head bowed. I followed him. I wanted to touch him, talk to him. But the space between us, no longer than his shadow, was full of boars and priests and a million voices of the dead, and there was no red bird waiting for me when I closed the door of our house behind me.

3 ～ THE
STRAW MAN

In England, for a while, the stories stopped. Things were happening to Frances, things that I didn't understand. In the junior high school, which was a jumble of reconstructed offices and barracks on the air base, we were shown movies about numerous strange changes occurring inside our bodies. But no one gave any clues to what was going on inside Frances's head. She seemed to burrow deep into herself like a hibernating bear. At noon, when we clustered on the edge of a ruined bomb shelter to eat our sandwiches, she rarely talked to anyone; she sat hunched over a book, dropping breadcrumbs between the pages as she read. Around us, girls were putting on lipstick, giggling over

boys, exchanging phone numbers. Frances just read. I
wanted desperately for her to be like everyone else, but she
only grew more strange. I was afraid of her slow, blank
moods that dragged her so far out of the world, made her so
different. I tried to make her remember how to tell stories,
but only bits and pieces of them surfaced in her mind, without beginnings or endings. Sometimes, though, when she
stared at the fog or the sunlight or the rain outside the windows during a boring class, I could sense her listening,
maybe for a story within her, in a language she had never
used before. Over a series of drizzly months her body went
entirely out of control.

"I have hair under my armpits," she announced glumly
one morning. She was getting heavy, too. She moved slug-
gishly, blinking at things from behind her glasses. "I'm
getting fat." She pulled down her nightgown and looked at
her breasts. "Well. I'm not flat anymore." She sat disconsolately, staring at nothing. I was angry, willing her to
move, but she didn't. Her face was round and boneless; her
eyes were round and blank. She seemed so hopeless. She
added wearily, "I hate school. Every time I look at a chocolate bar I break out. I'd run away to sea if I didn't have
breasts."

"What?"

"Or I'd be a musketeer. Or walk down the Grand Trunk
Road in India. But I'm trapped in an ugly body with
breasts."

I closed my eyes. The school bus was coming in half an
hour. The whole world was damp and soggy. I still had to
do my history homework. And she was still in her nightgown, blinking sadly like a turtle on her bed. But nothing

in our familiar world seemed compelling enough to interest her in moving. I said, feeling a little trapped, panicky in her motionlessness, "What do girls get to do?"

She got off the bed "Get rescued. Sit in a tower, waiting, looking at the world backward through a mirror."

"Waiting for what?" I asked, wanting to know if she knew what she was listening for. But she only picked her bra off a chairback and shrugged herself into it, sighing. Then I heard a high-pitched, eerie cry from the street outside that made Frances smile suddenly. It was a secret cry from a little wizened man, words cluttering together in a strange rhythm. As always, we argued over the cry.

"He's a rag-and-bone man; that's what he's saying."

"No," Frances insisted. "It's not rags and bones. It's something magic."

We argued so much I had to run through the graveyard and down the hill the church sat on, to the bus waddling slowly out of the fog.

We lived in a small town surrounded by a patchwork of fields. England seemed a placid country. Its skies were open; it had queens and no boars. It was incredibly old. In the graveyard of the church across the street from our house lay four-hundred-year-old bones. The church and our house were even older than that. It was there I realized that time didn't move in a straight line; it was a crooked river, constantly twisting back toward itself, pooling here and there into memory. I could walk down a street and see tumbled piles of brick that had once been houses destroyed in a war not twenty years before. Then the street itself would change, the past seeping up out of the ground in the shape of cobblestones worn smooth by centuries. Gypsies with no

74

past or future would rattle their wagons down the stones in search of a new hedge to camp by. The stones would curve beside the hunched doors of an eight-hundred-year-old cathedral, then turn to tar again, and continue on toward another memory. Even its writers were old—Kipling, Stevenson, Dickens, Shakespeare, Chaucer—stretching back to a past with no written language, when stories melted in and out of life the way time shifted along a street, until the lines between present and past, real and unreal, became blurred and dangerously unimportant.

Frances, I decided finally, had drifted into some crosscurrent of time. She didn't seem very interested in finding her way back. There was nothing in the history of the pioneers or beginning geometry that was strong enough to pull her mind out of its silence. She sat in buses staring out the windows as always, ignoring the constant chattering about football games, phone numbers, rallies and meetings, Mr. Kennedy and Mr. Nixon, some tempest brewing in Southeast Asia, and something called making out. Safe at home, she did her homework and read. She left me trying to straddle two worlds, one full of teen-agers and geometry problems, one full of Frances, neither of which made a great deal of sense to me.

She drifted so far out of time that finally, she pulled me off-balance. The milkman woke us up early one Saturday. His cartwheels needed oiling; they made an unearthly groan as his horse clopped down the street at dawn. Saturday was an open-market day. We rolled out of bed, got a couple of shillings' allowance, and went down to the town square to watch the booths being set up. Vendors sold dishes, fruit, toys, candy, pots and pans, clothes, old furniture, and big sweet soft buns full of currants that I loved. I bought some for breakfast, and then Frances dug through a crate full of old books at another booth. She opened one in the middle and stood very still, staring at it. There was a picture of the prow of a ship on a stormy sea, with a pale, naked figurehead smiling gently into the wind. I glanced at it. And suddenly, for a split second, the world disappeared.

I was on the ship. I felt it heave beneath my feet, and I could smell the strong salt wind. I heard the water smash against the side, and I felt it on my face. The wind was cold, and there were sea gulls crying. . . . Then the sky turned blue, and I stood on dirty pavement with a book in my hands.

The vendors were shouting, "Cherries, fresh, sweet cherries, come on ducks, 'ave an 'ot-cross bun, you'll never see such apples as these . . ." I felt strange.

"Frances."

"I'm here," she said.

"What was that?"

"I don't know. Something's happening."

"You shouldn't read so much. You don't even know what world you're in anymore."

Behind her glasses her eyes moved from the gray sea to focus on the world. "It's all right," she said after a moment. "Something's happening, but it will be all right."

She made the world disappear often after that. Sometimes I found myself inside a painting, sometimes in a phrase of music with regal horns or Spanish castanets; sometimes it just vanished around a splash of sunlight across the grass or a cluster of daffodils or a light rain at twilight. It made me want something, but I didn't know what. It made me restless and irritable. I went for long walks, tramping across muddy fields or down country roads, looking for something without a name, and always coming back without it. Frances was no help. She buried herself in books. When I nagged her out of one, she only said, "Wait." So I waited, feeling backward and blank as a mirror.

Finally, one day in November, she came out of hibernation. It had been raining off and on all day; at early evening the stars finally came out. I was in the living room, half reading, half watching a soap opera about men who swore and old ladies with hairnets who drank gin. The ads came on, and I turned a page. A torn piece of paper slid out from between the pages. I read it curiously. Then I read it again, and the second time it had an odd, compelling message between its lines, like a magical summons. Something in the blank shadows in the back of my brain stirred, like a tale coming to life. I read it slowly aloud. " 'I would like to be friends. If you would like, meet me in front of the church Sunday at seven.' " I had caught Frances's attention, her mind coming alive for the first time in months.

"Where the bloody hell did this come from?" I asked. "It fell out of *The Brothers Karamazov*. I was reading, and it just fell out."

She got me up off the floor. "Come on then. The quarterbells rang a few minutes ago. It's nearly time."

I sighed, turning off the telly. "I remember. Those boys that waited for their bus with us this morning. In uniform. Giggling and punching each other. The fat one eating toffee for breakfast—it was probably him."

"Maybe," she said softly. "But I don't think so. I think this is something else."

So I went. The church across the street was lit for some kind of service. It was huge, dark, and ancient; the narrow crescent moon was balanced on its dizzying spire. The round rose window was on fire from the light within. I kept my eyes on the window as I walked through the graveyard. I wasn't afraid of the dead at night, but the wet wind was whirling leaves against the stones and the iron railing, and the dry leaves were whispering like old bones. I heard the comforting drone of holy singing coming from the church. The big, flat gravestones seemed tilted toward the sound.

I went through it quickly, hugging myself in the chill. Rounding the church, I saw a figure in the light from the open doors. It was small, squat, and sitting in a wheelbarrow. Its legs and arms, in a garish suit, dangled bonelessly over the sides. A hat covered half its face; the rest was round as a pumpkin and pale as cheesecloth. It wore a black smile.

I stopped, my heart pounding. The singing—"A Mighty Fortress Is Our God"—was pouring out behind it. It was alone, staring at me and grinning. I felt a cold wind push me towards it, and I squealed, wondering what terrible sin Frances had committed, lusting after unknown writers of secret notes, in the doorway of an Anglican church.

Then I heard voices, kneelers banging, the shuffling sounds of a church emptying. People came out talking, laughing; a priest stood to one side of the devil in the wheelbarrow, shaking hands with his congregation. A boy righted the hat on the figure; its eyes were black, pupilless, staring at forbidden things. A handful of people gathered around it. Another boy said cheerfully, "A penny for the Guy? Who's got a copper then?"

A coin clanked into the wheelbarrow. Other boys joined him, lifted the limp white hands beseechingly. My heart went back to its normal size. Guy Fawkes. All the British autumn goblins came on November 5. We edged closer, through the stream of people. I could see the straw sticking out between the gloves and the sleeves, between the buttons of the coat. The boys in the church light looked rough and happy, wheedling coins from people they knew. I wanted to join them, touch the Guy, search for coins that had slid under its rump, but none of the faces was expecting us. Frances lingered at the edge of the light, waiting. An old lady threw a handful of coppers into the barrow; the boys dove for them, unsettling the straw man. They collected their coins, laughing. As they stood back, counting, someone tossed a match.

The Guy flamed. The boys leaped back, swearing breathlessly, still half laughing as the firelight swarmed over their faces. The flames ate the Guy's straw heart and then his bowels, as a ring of people congregated about him. Someone shouted, "Blimey, his legs are falling off," and jerked them back into the barrow. The face began to melt into the fire and the night. I watched, my mouth open. As the cheesecloth smile cracked and soared into the blackness, the ring of light widened, and I saw another face behind the Guy.

I couldn't see it clearly; light and shadow blurred it. The eyes seemed dark, smiling, with little flickerings of fire in them. They were drawing Frances. She took one step toward them, and then another. She was full of wonder; she seemed about to walk out of her short, pimply body to meet the flame of recognition. Then the Guy flared up in its death agony, the face vanished into fire.

"Who was that?" I demanded as I walked home through the graveyard. "Who?"

But Frances was back in her waiting tower, looking inward, and she only whispered, "I don't know yet. Wait." Then, for a while, she stopped talking.

Autumn darkened into winter. It was a strange season, such as I had never felt before. I was beginning to hear a language all around me that I had never been taught. The wind spoke it, whispering things into my head, tales of the past, of coming mysteries. I watched the oak trees in a wood nearby go bare. They knew something, I thought. They were old; they had been here before. I watched birds migrate, answering some command without words in their brains. I began to listen, as they listened, for words that made no sound, to watch for shapes that were masks, hollows around other shapes. Mushrooms bloomed like messages overnight, saying, Watch. Wait. The mystery is here. The holly, bright, shiny green among all the grayness, meant something, as the blazing straw of the Guy, imprisoned in his buttons and gloves, had meant something. But nobody told me what.

I biked out to the oak woods one afternoon between rainstorms. I sat on a damp log under dripping trees, trying to figure out what it was I wanted. There seemed no language for it, and yet it had something to do with everything around me: the great oak trees with their cold, tormented boughs, the stone walls patterning the fields, the mysteries of time, frozen into old churches, gravestones, and something even older, which was as elusive as the smell of a stone and as secret as the rustling behind me in the underbrush. My brain puzzled with the rustling. It was probably a crow poking among the dead leaves. But I didn't want to turn around and look, I realized suddenly, because if I looked, the mystery would be solved and the hundred possibilities rushing into my head would cease to exist. What kinds of tales drifted out of the English past to roam among the oak trees? I thought of the two faces of the straw man. One was a joke, a funny mask, covering up its other face, making it safe for people just coming out of church, so they could laugh and throw coins and forget. The other face was the mystery. The piece of a story that had wakened Frances's mind out of its stupor. The face of fire and danger. Things had two faces, I decided. There were statues of God, and then there was God, who was a feeling. There were mushrooms at my feet, which were real and possibly poisonous; then there were fairy rings of mushrooms. There were toads, and then there were toads that turned into princes. A real face, and an imaginary face. There was a rustling behind me that was probably a crow. But it might be an old woman out of a tale, come to tell one of the two sisters what she was doing sitting on a damp log on a soggy day, listening to a rustling in her heart. Two sisters. Two faces . . . I shivered suddenly and stood. The cold twilight wind was rousing. My thoughts had tangled into knots; I didn't know what I was thinking, or seeing, or smelling. Nothing made any sense, except my own want-ing, filling me like a dark cloud. The crow behind me startled up, squawking above my head. I looked up. The oak trees, which I had thought were barren, were wearing little beards or cobwebs in their branches. I caught a low branch, hoisted myself up, and tugged at a beard. It came loose easily: a tangle of soft leaves and pearl green berries.

I felt the tangle in my brain ease a little. Mistletoe. It was another message. Not everything was dead. Something was coming. The holly had pointed toward it, and now the mistletoe. Christmas. Christmas in England. It seemed to belong there, more than it had belonged in Arizona. In England the earth knew it was coming.

A few days later the autumn rains melted into the dead white calm of winter. I saw the first snowfall that I could remember. I stood inside the warm house, watching the silent white fall that slowly covered the grass, the walks, the street, the graves. I was sure the world had stopped, that we were becalmed at last between forevers, and our only future lay in the slow, mute messages of the earth.

The few weeks before Christmas seemed interminable. Every Sunday the priest wore purple; the Gospels spoke of signs and wonders and the coming of a prophet. A wreath of candles with purple ribbons on them flamed near the altar, marking the passage of weeks. We sang "Joy to the World," "There Is a Rose 'Ere Blooming," "We Three Kings of Orient Are," and "God bless the Master of this house, and the Misteress also, and all the little children who round the table go." The ground stayed white, sometimes thick and crunchy, sometimes slushy, almost melting. The stores decorated their windows with colored lights, angels' hair, pasteboard St. Nicks, with ruddy cheeks and pipes. Our kitchen smelled of spices, cookies, Christmas pudding, the funny British version of fruit cake, which my mother steamed on the stove in a small washtub. Packages began arriving from overseas; we got a tree to put them under. It was huge, dark, massing the corner of the living room where the TV used to be. I leaned next to it when no one was looking, smelled its needles, its dark sap, the lingering of cold and wind in its boughs. I nailed mistletoe in every doorway until my father laughed and called me a pagan. I puzzled over that word in silence. It meant something beyond the barbarians in the Bible who worshiped golden calves and slew the Jews. Looming over the silent, cold night journey of three kings under a midnight sky, and the child-God who created the universe, resting upon straw in a stable with His Virgin Mother beside Him, was a straw figure, smiling and drawing everything into its flames.

Friends from the air base came for high tea on Christmas Eve. We ate scones, crumpets, sizzling hot sausages in crisp dough, sponge cake, raspberry jelly roll, liver pâté sandwiches, cheese pennies, and Christmas pudding. Later, after everyone had left, I lay on the living-room floor, too full to move, listening to the noises of stone and wood around us as the house settled for the night. There were a few embers left in the fireplace, sparkling to flame now and then at a draft. The house darkened. I dozed, hearing my parents' footsteps vaguely in my sleep. They came downstairs, went out the front door quietly to midnight mass. I moved to curl up on the window seat. When I slept and opened my eyes again, Frances was with me, and the room was full of softly pulsing shadows.

She was expecting something. I smelled a mystery as tangible as the smell of fire, of cloves and nutmeg, of the snow covering the world. The stars were huge, as carefully placed as ornaments. Between them, within the deep blackness, wings rustled, words beyond hearing were spoken. Somewhere shepherds on a frosty hillside were waking to a golden light. The King of Kings, Lord of Lords was being born, and the earth was gathering Him into its stillness.

I slid the window up, let the wintry air tremble into the room. I wanted the night to last forever. I wanted the world to stop turning, to poise forever in the night sky, on the verge of wonder. As I gazed out at the snow and the stars, I saw a movement in the yard. Nothing was frightening that night; all things were possible. I leaned out the window. My breath was ghostly in the cold air. "There," Frances whispered. "There." Snow and shadow moved among the trees. Something was coming, the thing that I had wanted. . . . Moonlight touched it, drew it clear. I saw the dark eyes, liquid, secret, and I breathed in something that wasn't air but longing. A great stag gathered itself out of the silence, moved slowly across our vision, white as frost, with antlers that branched into the moonlight like a crown of pure white fire.

It turned to look back at us before it faded out of sight. By then I was half out the window, the cold air burning in my throat. The church bells across the street broke the silence, ringing a joyous, wild midnight peal, and I jumped, banging my head on the sill. I could see hoofprints in the snow. I didn't know if I was waking or dreaming; I didn't know how to tell anyone what I had seen. I wanted someone else to see the fiery snow, the stillness that had built the stag out of itself. I paced the room, my head full of embers and pine needles, shadows and bells. I wanted to shout with frustration. There were too many visions in my body, too many feelings trapped in silence. Frances was very quiet. I stopped pacing finally and listened to her silence, which was like the silence of snow over the Christmas world. I knew then what I wanted to do. But I knew also that I didn't have the courage to turn visions into reality, to lose myself completely to such seductive dreams. One of us had to turn a face to the real world. So I made Frances take binder paper from a drawer, find a pencil. Slowly she began to draw the stag with words. The excitement and frustration left me, as though she were emptying the words out of me. She wrote until I was calm for the first time in months, drained of visions except in memory. I fell asleep then. I dreamed the stag had gone to Bethlehem, where the Christ child gazed back at it out of the stag's own secret, fiery eyes.

December ended; we went back to school in the harsh January weather. The snow froze into ugly ridges and imprints. Crows dead of cold made little stiff shadows on the white ground. Then it began to rain, long gray days sloshing with water from morning until night until I thought the world was going to drown. Frances had never stopped writing. Her long silence was broken; the stories came flooding out of her. She scribbled on binder paper on buses, in the kitchen when she was supposed to be doing her homework, at school when she got bored. I gave up even trying to persuade her to act normal; I was too fascinated. Then something started bothering me, some question in the back of my brain. For a while she ignored me, intent on her tales. Then her pencil began to slow. It stopped completely one day in midsentence.

"All right. All right."

"Where did the stag go? Look at the world. It's like an old shoe full of water. What about the fire? What about Guy Fawkes's eyes? I want to go where the stag went."

"You can't," she said shortly, and started writing again. But her pencil lead snapped. She leaned back tiredly. She was wrapped in an old sleeping bag because the house had a big fireplace only in the living room for heat, and the bedroom was cold.

"Why not?"

"Because." She was quiet for a long time, while I read through her stack of school paper full of stories. I finished finally, my head full of secret kingdoms, forests, wishes, all the stuff of fairy tales. I felt strange, satisfied, but bewildered.

"Who are all these princes? Where are the sisters?"

"Back in the house in the woods. They never leave."

"Why not?"

"They just don't. The sisters never leave the woods. The princess never leaves the tower. The queen leaves the castle only if she is going to run away to the woods and get married. So I had to use princes. It's in all the books."

"All those he's? He went there, he did this, he did that—"

"It's in the books," she said patiently. "I told you. Dickens, Dumas, Dostoevsky, Kipling, Stevenson, King Arthur. The men follow the stags."

"But," I said inarguably. "But." So she was silent again, chewing on her pencil.

86

She said finally, softly, with a strange kind of shame, "I can't hear their voices. I don't have their voices in my head. The women's voices. I have only the men's voices. That's all I can find."

"Alice in Wonderland fell down a rabbit hole."

"That story always scared me," she said glumly. She added after a while, "I don't even know how to try. The sea, horses, swords, dragons, songs, churches, magic words, ships, and stars—I don't have any other way to think about them. All the storytelling words belong to men."

"I don't care." I felt hot inside, blind and irritable, struck by something so light I couldn't feel pain, so fine I couldn't fight it, like spider webs hitting my face in the dark. "Make the sisters follow the stag."

"I'll try," she said, but her voice was unhappy. "But I don't know how it will end."

The rain fell relentlessly; the days passed into a soggy Lent. Priests wore purple again; the face of the crucified Christ was hidden; our house smelled of fish on Fridays. Frances gave up writing for Lent because she loved it so; I felt as if I were in a mild state of shock for six weeks, with all the stories piling up inside her and no place to come out. At school everyone was fidgety, short-tempered; we all were tired of looking at one another's face. Boys picked fights with each other in the hallways, with their teachers in empty classrooms. Frances sat like a lump in her classes, answering questions when asked, disappearing into a story in her head when no one demanded that she exist. The streets were gray, the fields were dead; the only animals I saw were miserable-looking sheep.

Finally, one day, I woke up to find the bright sun drizzling through the rain at dawn. The rain stopped; the sun kept shining, splitting bulbs, drawing crocuses and daffodils out of the garden, bringing out hard knots of buds on trees. The sour apple trees in the backyard, with their crabbed, twisted limbs, suddenly broke into blossom. I stood under them, unable to believe them, shaking their petals loose to shower into my eyes. The sheep stopped looking sodden. Bicycling through a herd on a back road, I watched lambs struck with spring, leap straight up in the air, as if they were trying to fly. Farmers started working their fields again, plowing, seeding. Birds jabbered in the ivy around my window in the morning. Winter had ended, but there was one last thing to do. For three hours on Friday we sat in a dim church, listening to the drag of a crucifix across the centuries, to the final pound of a nail, the last word, the roll of a stone across the tomb of the winter king.

Then, in the odd, quiet period between the end of things and the beginning of them, the two sisters left their house.

We walked together to the oak woods. The trees still looked bare from a distance, their branches flaring up like dark antlers, but when we stood under them, we could see the little buds of new green leaves beginning to open. The midlands sloped away from the woods, a crazy quilt of fields tucked over the world. An apple orchard blossoming in the distance lay like a soft white pillow against the quilt. Beyond it was a church spire. Beyond that, tiny, smoking factory stacks. Then the flat, misty circle of the world.

I sat down on a log. A bushy gray squirrel stopped to

stare at me. Frances said to it, "Okay. The two sisters left their house in the woods. Both of them this time. They put on their best clothes and packed all their food and locked the door because they didn't know when they would be home. Or if."

"What do you mean, 'if'?"

"Well. This is a story without an ending. They started walking at morning. Animals followed them: birds, squirrels, rabbits, deer. They ate blackberries and drank clear stream water. At noon the animals started to leave them, to go back to their own homes. The sisters traveled onward. The beautiful one picked flowers and twined them through her hair. The ugly one, who couldn't talk, looked at all the red birds passing by to see if one of them was hers. But none of them was. The sun began to set; the forest grew very quiet. The small things living in the trees started showing their faces. But nothing tried to harm the sisters. Finally, just as the full moon rose, they saw the stag.

"He was standing just across a little stream. The water was silver with moonlight. He was like moonlight, like white fire. He stood still, his head just raised, water running in little diamonds out of his mouth. His eyes were full of light, and his antlers were burning. His breath, when he breathed out, was a silver mist that glittered down into the water. He was so beautiful that the beautiful sister wanted to give him her roses and the ugly sister wanted to speak.

"He turned, walked away into the dark trees, and they followed him. Sometimes they had to run. He was always ahead of them, just ahead of them, like a silver streak in the dark. The sisters tripped over roots and skinned their

89

hands. They tore their best clothes, and the beautiful sister lost all her roses. The ugly one started to cry out in pain. Her voice was ugly, like the crow's, but it was her voice. When dawn came, the stag leaped into the rising sun and disappeared.

"The sisters stopped then. They were lost in the deep woods. They had lost their food and their shoes. They were tired and dirty. They both started to cry because they were hungry and they didn't know how to get home. After a while they stopped crying. They found wild apples and mushrooms and nuts and had a good breakfast. Then they felt better. The ugly sister braided the beautiful sister's hair, so it wouldn't get in her way. The beautiful sister taught the ugly one a word. The sun rose higher. They decided that since the stag had leaped into the sun, they should follow the sun.

"The sun led them to the stars at twilight, and the stag appeared again. He ran faster this time, and the sisters had to run all night to keep him in view. This time they were chased by bears and robbers, who wanted to cut off the beautiful sister's hair. But she shouted at them that they had no time for bears, no time to be afraid, and ran faster. The stag was the only light in the world. All around them was the dark; above them was the moon, white and fiery as the stag. They followed the stag into dawn. Then, when the stag melted into the sun, they both fell down on the ground and lay without moving, until leaves drifted over them, as if they were dead.

"But they weren't. They woke up near twilight and found a stream to drink out of and dip their feet into. They had no food, but they weren't hungry. They could only think of the stag. There was something in him they wanted. Something kept them running after him, though they didn't know what, and they didn't know if they would die before they ever found out. They sat by the stream and waited, not saying anything. And as it grew dark, the beautiful sister was as quiet as the ugly one, and the ugly one's face as shadowed and silvered by moonlight as the beautiful sister's face.

"The stag appeared, leaped over the stream and over their heads with one powerful leap, and the sisters got up and followed him. This time he ran as fast as he could. They followed him, even though the air they breathed seemed to turn as heavy as ice inside them and their bruised feet no longer felt the ground. And this time the stag seemed to grow blurred in his flight until sometimes he didn't always look like a stag. This made the sisters run faster. The ugly sister felt words coming into her throat, and the beautiful sister's hair came unbound and spread behind her like a path of gold in the dark.

"Finally, the whole world was gold with dawn. The stag gave a mighty leap, but this time the ugly sister called out to him, and he missed the sun. He came back to earth and turned slowly toward them. And then they saw what he was."

I waited. The story just stopped, the way the stag stopped. The silence left me staring at a beetle pushing its way through the leaves. I waited a little longer. Then I yelled, "Frances, what was he?"

She didn't answer. A spring wind rattled through the oak

branches, telling an ending I couldn't hear. "Frances," I shouted, but the wind whispered only one word: "Wait."

Her stag ran through my dreams all night. Bells woke me, an Easter peal from the church. It was barely dawn; I was full of sleep and stag dreams and the thought that God had risen from the dead. Frances said impatiently, "Come on." I didn't know where we were going. I just got dressed, to see where her wordless feelings led. She couldn't even wait for me to put my shoes on. So I went down barefoot, with my blouse buttoned all wrong, into the morning.

The sun had just risen. The birds were waking in the trees, surrounding us with invisible voices. The grass was sunlit, but still cool, sparkling with night. I thought we were going to the oak woods, but Frances led me across the street into the graveyard. The graves were rimmed with light. I gave up asking Frances questions and just followed her around the church to the front of it where we had seen the Guy with his eyes. The stag was waiting.

His eyes were a man's eyes. His face was a stag's. He was crowned with antlers the color of oak. He was naked, as though he had just been born with the morning. He was very tall, very still. He stood in front of the church, the Stagman. His skin was the color of oak. The muscles in his arms and thighs and belly were smooth and hard. His eyes were hard, glittering with light, smiling. The sun blazed down over him, setting him to flame. His hands opened, big, brown, opening to light. His bones and skin and muscle flowed together as though he had been carved out of one great oak trunk. But he was alive, breathing in the sun, fiery, beautiful, and dangerous, coming out of nowhere into Frances's story.

I couldn't speak. I couldn't move. I didn't know what he was, God or devil, good or evil. I wanted to cry or yell at Frances for waking something like that out of the past around us, putting it into my mind. *Now that you've got him,* I wanted to shout, *what am I going to do with him?* Most of all, I wanted to run. But I couldn't take my eyes off him. After a while I stopped wanting to run.

4 ～ TWILIGHT PEOPLE

Iceland. A word so cold I could feel it. It wouldn't melt in the dusty California sunlight across my desk. A Norseman, striding across glaciers in fur-lined boots with tufts of fur spangled, gently singing with ice. The blue glacier of a sky ringing the apex of the world.

My mouth was already coated with morning dust. I shifted, unsticking my legs from the chair. Then I assumed the virtues of the desk: stolid, motionless, vaguely scarred. I wore uniform blue and white once again. My face felt flat and expressionless as wood. My mind was fragmented into a hundred thoughts. One thought sucked at the sweet, unbearable ice word. One ran to the rhythms of Sister

Catherine's voice, picked shadows, scents, impressions out of doctrine as old as my memory. One noted Frances's fuzzy calves above her regulation socks. Children's socks that little girls folded down toward patent-leather shoes. She always forgot to shave her legs.

One thought flinched from the burning glance of chrome and glass from the cars passing below. One heard the cadence of a question in Sister Catherine's voice, kept my body still as desk wood until another voice began to murmur. A breath of stagnant, tarry air came in suddenly through the window. My mind shrank together, rolled like a marble into the bottom of a colorless bowl.

Adrift in the classroom, among rows of white backs, I tried magic talismans to escape. Iceland. Ocean spray. Galactic void. Longship. Cathedral. Quasar. In the limp spring, spells failed me. Time, history, the martyrdom of saints failed me. Red velvet, Scaramouche, Tirnan Og jangled senselessly together. My nose itched, but if I moved, I would no longer be a desk. Agnes Harte's gleaming shoes shifted into my vision; she was rising to answer a question. Agnes went to mass in the mornings and to chapel at three-fifteen, when the others jammed the bathrooms to put on eye make-up. Agnes knew all the answers.

"And you, Frances, do you agree with her? Frances? Frances!"

Frances jumped. Her elbow hit the desk edge hard; she came up rubbing it, her mouth pinching into a straight, pained line. The full, airless light hit her from the windows. Her white shoes were scuffed; the pleats in her skirt hung as uninspired as the air. She cleared her throat.

"Yes?"

"Yes, what?"

Capital punishment? Communism? The Ecumenical Council? "Yes, Sister."

Someone chuckled. Frances stared straight ahead. I had no idea what we were discussing. Then an odd rag of phrase and tone my mind had snagged at came back to me: "Because even that small, it is already part of God's plan. . . ." Abortion?

"Yes, I agree." The words came out of Frances flat, like a computer print-out. "No one has the right to take a child's life before it is born. God makes the child, and its death belongs to God." She sat down with a slight thump. There was a brief silence, as if all the minds in the room had suspended thought. An odd, quizzical expression on Sister Catherine's face made me wonder suddenly what we had been talking about. But as she opened her mouth to comment, the bell rang.

One more class, one more . . . I raised an armload of books to my chest and eased toward the door. Justine Cramer's blond head got in the way of my vision, and Mary Ellen Evens, reaching in front of me, grabbed Justine's arm as we filed out.

"Justine, lend me your history questions."

"I didn't do them," Justine said impatiently. Mary Ellen's voice rose. Her eyes were round, perpetually unprepared, perpetually alarmed.

"You didn't do them either? Nobody did them. Ster Hilary will have kittens. We're supposed to discuss them with our books shut."

"Well, we'll have to discuss them with our mouths shut."

"But, Justine, nobody—"

"Do I care? Do I give two damns?" Then she wrenched herself out of Mary Ellen's clutch. "Frances. Frances always does her homework."

Sensing trouble, as usual, with Frances, I let her handle it. There wasn't much I could do for her those days, besides seeing she got her homework done and her shoes polished occasionally, since her imagination was invading my mind, and her blank face and shy voice were constantly overwhelming all my good intentions. She was walking quickly as always, with her head bent. She had expert powers of camouflage. In the hallways she turned into a uniform; in the yard at lunchtime she turned into a bench. She had been so hopeless in PE, with basketballs bouncing off her head, that they had let her drop it; for that class at least she had mastered the art of disappearing entirely. Her head jerked as she became aware of her escort; she glanced from side to side, her mouth shaping the nervous smile that I hated.

"Frances, you've got to help us," Mary Ellen hissed. There was no talking in the halls. "Let us have your history homework. Please—just five minutes."

The smile faded. Frances glanced at Justine. Then her head bent again; she shook it.

"Please! We're not going to copy it—just read it. It's not like cheating."

"Mary Ellen Evens, will you please be quiet?" one of the hall monitors said monotonously.

"We'll get into trouble, both of us, if we can't discuss—Oh, come on, Frances—God, you act like it's a mortal sin—"

Frances's face burned furiously with embarrassment. She was disappearing, wincing somewhere, like a snail coiling into itself. In another moment Mary Ellen would be arguing with a shell. Then Frances's face turned toward Justine, away from Mary's derision, and Justine said sharply, "Mary Ellen, shut up."

"Jesus Christ, Justine," Mary Ellen squealed indignantly, "you're the one who said to ask her—"

"Mary Ellen Evens." A black slab of authority blocked their way. "Report to your homeroom after school for detention. Justine Cramer, you have a demerit for talking in the halls."

Justine tossed her hair, as she always did when she was groping for an answer or making a swift decision. "She wasn't talking."

"Who? Mary Ellen? I could hear her quite clearly, and so, I imagine, could the old sisters in the convent and the priests in the rectory across the street."

"No, Sister, I mean—" But Frances was no longer beside her; she was ahead, opening the door to their next class. She had passed, invisible as the Holy Ghost, through the glare of the dean of students. I heard Justine mumble as the door closed, "Nothing, Sister."

During the acid lecture Sister Hilary gave us for not doing our homework, Frances did her usual spell of invisibility. The wrinkles in her blouse were immovable. Her head was bent at the same angle as the heads around her; her hands lay flat on her desk. Her knees were well covered with gray. Her upper arms were pallid; her short hair looked as indecisive as the rest of her. She became effortlessly unremarkable. Yet in the lank afternoon even her strong magic turned against her. Sister Hilary pounced on

98

her; she rose, plump, soft-voiced, yet somehow etched sharply back into existence.

"Frances Stuart, did you do your homework?"

"Yes, Sister."

"Then why don't you raise your hand and discuss the questions? You never talk in this class, and you know that group discussion is a quarter of your grade. I want you to raise your hand three times today. Whether you have anything to say or not. And I'm sure that you do."

Frances sat down again slowly. She swallowed. Her hands came together, locked, and she didn't move again. I felt a thrill of calculation run through the class, and I knew, with all the silent betting going on, there was no way that Frances could charm the class into forgetting she was there. Sister Hilary requested briskly that we turn to page 233. I flipped to it, sat staring at a diagram of the power structure of the Kremlin. Sister Hilary's voice dwindled, into something heard through the wrong end of an ear trumpet. The flat white plains of the book margins, the barren pages, rolled across my mind in a mighty incantation: tundra. For a moment a silence spread across my mind, broken only by the thin, bell-like voices of wild flowers.

"Justine Cramer," Sister Hilary said, and Justine broke my silence, breathing as she got to her feet, "Oh, hell."

The room was charged with Frances's motionlessness. Without even blinking, she had drawn about her a static of attention. Curious glances, whisperings, restlessness ran in an undercurrent to Sister Hilary's lecture. Even Sister Hilary seemed to be listening beneath her own words for something else: the voices of wild flowers in the tundra, maybe, or Frances's voice.

99

Five minutes before the bell rang, Sister Hilary exploded. "Frances Stuart!"

The back of Frances's neck jerked. She moved her hands apart, gripping the edge of her desk before she stood. "Yes, Sister." Her voice was monotonous. Sister Hilary's history book snapped shut.

"Do you know why you refuse to raise your hand in class?" The wire-rimmed glasses flashed a white light at Frances, and she swallowed.

"Yes, Sister." It was a statement, not a question, but Sister Hilary intoned a word like an incantation against Frances's magic and ran over her voice.

"Pride."

Ten centuries of theology and a fallen angel whose name was light stood behind the word. It was a nice try, but Sister Hilary could not have known how many basketballs had bounced off the top of Frances's head or how many answers in her soft, scratchy voice had never been heard.

"Pride. You're afraid of being wrong," Sister Hilary said with satisfaction. "Good God, we all make mistakes. We're human. Half you people in here make fools of yourselves every time you stand up. It's nothing to be ashamed of. Now sit down. We have a few minutes left, and I want to see your hand in the air and hear your voice before the end of class."

Frances sat, with a swift economy of movement that ended in such a familiar position it cast doubt as to whether she had stood up at all. No one looked directly at her. No one moved. Feet were together; skirts fanned out identically over the sides of chairs. A pencil rolled down a desk; a hand slapped it still. Frances stared, as always, at the blank face of her desk.

"Until 1917 Russia was ruled by the czars; the events of that year changed the structure of the government. To recap today's lecture, who was the last czar of all the Russias, and what took place in 1917 that cost him his throne?" Sister Hilary paused. Like her class, she seemed to be gazing into nothingness. "Can anyone tell me?"

The second hand on the clock went into spasms, jerking reluctantly across each second. The sunlight seemed painted on the carpets. The air was dusty with seconds ticked away. Neither Frances nor Sister Hilary looked at each other; their heads were slightly bowed. Someone, nerveless as the clock, hissed one word at Frances's pallid back: "Frances-raiseyourhand!" The wrinkles in Frances's blouse gave no sign of hearing. Then Justine Cramer made a sound like a growl in the back of her throat, and her hand shot into the air with such imperativeness that half the class jumped.

I couldn't see her face, but there must have been an expression on it that not even Sister Hilary could ignore. When called on at last, Justine picked her words precisely. The bell rang halfway through her answer; she dropped a word in the middle and bent to pick up her books. Her face was bright pink, as if she had washed it in strawberries. In the clatter that followed, Sister Hilary's voice sounded as monotonous as Frances's.

"Frances, see me after school."

I made her talk on the way home. I had to make her, or her feelings would be so tangled and confused in her silence that I wouldn't know what I was feeling. The high school was three pink stucco buildings on half a city block. The oak trees around it dropped hot, dusty gold-brown leaves, for it was early autumn. From the tiny inner courtyard we heard the sound of a late volleyball game. Frances was no better at that than at basketball. Someone had thrown a wine bottle against the iron fence; the pieces gleamed with knife edges of sunlight. I kicked them into the gutter.

"Tell me what she said."

Frances shrugged. She was carrying Latin, history, algebra, biology, some music, *Lord of the Flies,* and her notebooks, so her shrug was sluggish. She didn't want to remember the word, but I made her. She had to drag the word out of her silence into daylight, or it would haunt the dark in the back of my mind, unspoken and growing more terrible and confusing. She had to tell me if it was true or not. In this piece of the world, autumn was only a deepening of the shades of summer: dust, ivory, straw. The sicksweet smell of a cannery nearby drifted through the air; the stars at night were little pinpricks in the dark. We were back in the country where we belonged, in a city with old walnut and pepper trees, tired houses, and air the sun beat to a still, pale gold.

"Tell me what she said. Say the word."

Her head was bent, but she wasn't crying; her voice was dry. "It's like the bottle."

"What?"

"The broken bottle. She was wrong. It's not pride. It's pieces of the broken bottle, hurting inside. . . . She wants me to be a machine. A gray piece of machine, sitting with other gray pieces. I wear the uniform; I do my homework; I do everything they tell me. But if I stand up and say their words, nothing but their words, then that's all they'll ever hear from me. I'll be a face saying their words, and they'll think—they'll be happy with me, they'll never guess how much I hurt. . . . Some days it hurts when someone smiles at me. Because they make me real, seeing me, and it scares me." She was silent, crossing a street. A warm wind puffed dead leaves; they scrabbled after us like mice. Frances's head came up a little. "Listen. Listen to them. They're like people, twilight people; they have a different story . . . full of night colors; the story begins when the real day ends. . . ." Her feet quickened slightly, following the tale.

"Say what she said."

"No."

"Say the word."

Her face pinched. "She said—when I first came, I was so still. Pale and still. Listening. Not moving. So many things touched me, hurting, so I didn't move. They thought I was—"

"What word?"

"I was—"

"What word?"

"They thought I was retarded." She swallowed. Then she laughed, a dry laugh full of dust. "In that school. Learning Latin and algebra." Then she stopped, walked face first into a big, gnarled pepper tree, and twisted her body against it. She tried to disappear into it. But she was solid in that world, on the cracked sidewalk, with the sunlight on her back and books in her arms. She came back slowly, her face marked with tree bark. "Someday I won't be shy," she said. "It won't hurt to live. I swear it. I'll do it. I swear it." She seemed a little demented, coming out of the tree, but I had to believe her. I had no other hope but her hope.

I walked in silence past the apartment house where the old people sat talking together on rusty garden chairs or walking slowly up and down a patch of straggly lawn. A big car fishtailed past; boys leaned out the window, shouting things in English and Spanish. Little kids in blue uniforms with sailor blouses ran past; they were from the grammar school across the street. A man in shoes cut open across the tops stopped meandering down the sidewalk to stare. "Hey, girl," he said. "Hey. You want to go to a movie?" I ducked my head and walked faster. When I glanced back, he was still staring, shimmering a little, like a mirage in the heat.

"When twilight comes," Frances said, "he'll be in another story." She tilted her head up to look at the blazing sky through the limp, dry leaves. "Autumn. Smell it."

"All I smell is car exhaust."

"Apples hanging in trees, wet with evening rain . . ."

"That was England."

"You go outside to smell them. Into the darkening sky. The grass is wet. The back porch lights the rain clinging to the apples. The grass is long and wet. It smells of secrets. A wind rises; you hear dry leaves scatter across the sidewalk, and you turn, but they're not leaves. . . . And your heart says: 'Oh, of course, that's what they have to be if they're not leaves. . . .'"

"You have to write a paper on the Russian Revolution." She sighed. "Tomorrow."

"No. Tonight. Plus all that algebra."

"No. Not tonight."

"Yes. Plus thirty pages of *Lord of the Flies*. Plus the Latin vocabulary. Plus—"

"All right. All right. All right."

"You know what else she said."

"That I should be making straight A's so I can get into a good university. If I study all the time, when am I going to write? I'll give them just enough." She scuffed through leaves; her voice was stubborn. "Just enough. Latin verbs, Russian Revolutions, equations . . . the twilight belongs to me."

"Why are you so shy?" Sister Anne Marie, the dean of students, asked Frances the next day. "Sister Hilary says you won't talk in her class." Frances blushed and mumbled something at her toes. Sister Anne Marie was short, dark-eyed, lively; she was working on her Ph.D. in history. She ignored Frances's mumble and scanned her class schedule for the next year. "Why are you dropping Latin?"

"I don't like it."

"If you have four years of Latin, you'll better your chances of getting into a good university. I advise you to keep taking it."

Frances's voice slid back into her throat. "I don't like Latin. I'd rather take French."

"French is fine, of course, but Latin is a basic language of scholars. I would strongly advise you to keep up with it." She leveled her black eyes at Frances. She was all in black; her straight eyebrows were formidable. She quoted Santayana at us the first day of class. She was small, though, and quick, like a girl, and she lost her temper and laughed easily. Frances wanted to please her. But I knew what she was thinking: *puella, puellae, puellarum.* What kind of word was that for a girl? French had strange, flowing sounds, and living women spoke it, not dead Caesars. So she stood shaking her head, pallid and solid, until Sister Anne Marie lowered her pen to the paper, frowning. "All right. I'll approve this, but I heartily disapprove." She signed my schedule, and we left the Holy of Holies. There were half-moons of sweat under Frances's arms; she didn't say anything.

"Are you going to the mixer?" Diana Halfax asked Frances as we pulled books for our next class out of our lockers. "You should come—everyone's going. The St. Andrews guys are really cute." She was slender and pretty, with dark hair in a long braid down her back. She had green eyes and an angular, smiling face. Frances looked at her hoplessly a moment. Her hair was springing out in various strange directions; her face looked as if she had swallowed a chocolate factory. She pulled out her algebra book wearily.

"No."

"Come on. Give it a try."

"Not this time. Anyway, I can't dance."

"You don't have to dance, you just wiggle. Oh, Frances. Why are you so shy?"

"Frances," Justine said behind us, catching up with us in the street after school. Frances turned, startled at the sound of her name. They looked at each other a moment, Frances puzzled and wary, Justine hesitant, her brows angled upward. She was tall, slender, nearly beautiful, with her pale

hair and her restless, angry face. She fit compactly into her
body; she knew how to manage her joints and bones. Even
her knees were pretty, flushed with sunburn under their
tan. She had rolled her skirt up to let them show and put
on eye shadow. The color was uneven; she had put it on
to annoy. Frances, who wore her own body with weary
resignation, said nothing, waited. Justine spoke finally,
without her usual assuredness, as if she didn't quite know
what she was talking to.

"I just wanted to tell you—that was a gutsy thing you did,
standing up to Hilary like that." Frances made a sound in
her throat. Justine paused a second; when Frances made no
more civilized noise, she added, "I was wondering why you
did it. I mean, why—" She stuck and flicked a hand through
her hair, impatient with herself. Without moving, Frances
had taken a step backward. Justine reached out to her,
touching her, holding her still. "I mean—oh, shit, that nun
pisses me off, too, but you made me wonder then, when
you do talk, what you say."

Frances's eyes went wide. Justine's touch was a terrible
magic. But she didn't know what she was doing yet. She
was asking for the sun to fall, a stone to speak, for a different voice to come out of Frances's mouth. As it was, I felt
the hot breeze run cold under my arms, and I wanted to
pull my shadow out from under Justine's oxfords. I said,
feeling trees shift into shape around me, the hard sidewalk,
and the hot blue sky, "No." But Frances was simply silent,
and Justine's hand slipped away finally.

"I'm sorry," she said, but she wasn't. She looked at
Frances a moment longer, curiously. "I mean, you know,
after a couple of years around here, you get to know the

way people think. Agnes Harte is holy; Mary Ellen's an idiot; Christine is brainy; I'm a rebel. You're quiet. But you're a rebel, too. I never knew that." She paused a moment longer, then touched Frances again briefly and laughed. "I'm also obnoxious. You can ignore me. But I still like what you did." She turned, shaking her hair into the wind, while Frances watched.

"First you're retarded," I said. "Then you're a rebel." But she didn't speak to me either. I was afraid.

We were singing at a white mass—the mass of death for a child. The church was half-shadowed with candlelight. Tongues of fire burned above our gloved hands. The small coffin stood in the main aisle, with wreaths of lilies, white roses, white ribbons on it. I didn't know whose child it was that brought us out of our classrooms to sing at its funeral. We sang the Magnificat: "My soul doth magnify the Lord, my spirit hath rejoiced in God my Savior . . ." Mary's song to her unborn child. Her statue rose out of the shadows at one side of the altar, blue, white, crowned with gold. A heart of fire shaped by votive lights stood at her feet; all the candles were lit. She held lilies and red roses in her hands. On the other side of the altar stood a winged man thrusting a spear toward a serpent's heart, smiting the darkness with red, green, white. The Archangel Michael, thrusting Satan out of heaven. The tabernacle gleamed gold on the altar, with its small door behind which God, in the form of moon-white wafers, dwelled. Behind the altar the God-man stood on a billow of cloud, crowned with thorns and light. His lean, wounded hands were open to receive a dead child's soul. The waxy white of lilies, the pure white of the altar cloths, the lustrous, glowing white of beeswax shone through a dusk of candlelight and sorrow. Father Pearson moved through the twilight world, murmuring, the chalice of blood glittering in his hands.

"Pax domini sit semper vobiscum."

His open hands encompassed us all, wove us into the fire and incense, the gold, the music, the still saints watching us, the hands above him, open to encompass the world. The doors opened behind us; sunlight streaked down the aisle. Four seniors lifted the coffin; we followed it, still singing, out into the hot, stagnant air, down the steps where the man with cut shoes, lounging on the bottom steps, stared at the coffin and took a deep swig out of his bottle of Ripple.

We filed quietly back into the schoolyard. "What's a hobbit?" somebody murmured. I couldn't hear Justine's answer. But I saw then what she was carrying instead of her missal. The question hung pleasantly in the back of my mind, something to which there might be many strange answers.

The delicate colors of Indian summer were washed away by soggy rains that made the dead leaves stick like corn-flakes. Frances started writing a novel about a mythical kingdom like Ruritania; she had been reading *The Prisoner of Zenda*. Then she discovered a book she carried with her for a week. She read it before school, at lunchtime, in the bathroom, at night when she was supposed to be asleep. The wet world took on a dreamlike sheen: geese flying in their high, smooth wedges above a fingernail moon in the damp sky spoke of lands without boundaries; the observatory on top of a distant hill was a castle; roads in the gentle mountains we crossed to get to the sea might lead anywhere, curving into timeless forests where unicorns slipped from moon shadow to moon shadow and griffins screamed.

"Unicorns," I said. "In California." But she ignored pink stucco and red tile roofs and created quests. "For knights," I said, but she ignored me. A character was growing out of her pen; the horned god, the Stagman, rustling among the wet twisted branches of California oak, became more human as he traveled through her mind. He bared his face, brought it, fine, wild, and vulnerable, into human view. She clothed him, armed him, sent him into the world to find his name. She sat hunched on her bed at night, pale and quiet, poring over him, her pen moving steadily, while true stars above her head gave their faint cries of light for her attention, and in the darkness of her forests things crept beyond her knowledge.

"*The Once and Future King,*" Justine cried, prowling before religion, pouncing on it where it was sandwiched between Frances's notebooks. Frances blushed. "I love that book. Look at this, Debbie—look what Frances is reading. It's about King Arthur."

"Who?" Debbie said, practicing a cheer in mid-aisle.

"King Arthur, dodo. You know—knights, quests, magic animals, Camelot—"

Debbie grunted tolerantly. She spread her legs into a V, touched the floor between her feet with her palm without bending her knees, and straightened with her hands on her hips. "Must be good. I don't read fairy tales. You coming to the game tonight? We're trying to get perfect attendance."

"I hate games."

"Oh, Justi-ine."

"I do. I think they're fascist." She gave *The Once and Future King* back to Frances and sat down in the desk in front of her to talk. "Have you read *The Hobbit?*"

Frances's set face moved after a moment. "What's a hobbit?"

"They're little men with hairy feet." She ignored Debbie's snicker, contemplating Frances. "It takes place in an imaginary world. I like imaginary worlds—"

"Justine, you're in my chair, move your bod," Liz Hartshoren, class secretary, said briskly.

"Shut up. I'm having a conversation."

"Why are volleyball games fascist?" Debbie asked indignantly.

"Weren't you sad at the end of *The Once and Future King?*" Justine said. "I cried."

Frances stared at her, amazed. "You cried?"

"Did you?"

"A little." She added, "I liked the writing. I could never write like that." She realized what she had said then, and her face closed as an anemone does when you touch it. Justine's face changed.

"Is that what you do? At noontime sometimes? When you look like you're doing homework?" Frances was trying to hide in her hair; Justine put a hand on her desk. "I write, too. Song lyrics, mostly. Music, sometimes, for my guitar. I wrote one about *The Hobbit*. About going down strange roads, searching for—"

"Justine," Liz said, exasperated. "I need my desk."

"I want to know why volleyball games are fascist."

"Speaking of guitars, people," Hilary Adams said heftily, "look at this." She spread a newspaper under our noses. Four young men with longish hair and impassive faces gazed out at us.

Debbie gave a squeal, as if someone had handed her a teddy bear. "Oh, my God. The Beatles."

"Girls, please," Sister Theresa said from her desk. "Watch your language and moderate your voices. They're only musicians."

We settled down, after a while, to learn about sex. It wasn't very interesting. There was a short cartoon I had seen before about an egg flowing down from fluffy clouds of ovaries and a film about two teen-agers which left us with the impression that kissing caused pregnancy. We had a discussion about the church's position about sex and sin. Justine asked if French kissing was a mortal or a venial sin. Sister Theresa sighed, but she tackled the problem.

"Kissing itself is not a sin. But the arousal of desires could lead to a potentially dangerous situation. Keep your mouth closed, and avoid temptation. Besides," she added distastefully, "I don't see why you would want somebody else's tongue in your mouth."

I agreed with her. Debbie raised her hand.

"How long can a kiss last before it turns into a sin?"

"Oh," Sister said tiredly, "about three seconds."

I couldn't sleep that night. The Stagman wandered through the darkness behind my eyes, on his lonely quest. He spoke to falcons and to holy hermits. He stared at the flat, endless blue sky, without a sign in it to mark his path.

He was not yet human; he was searching for the path out of his godhead. He was at once fierce and gentle, with no past, belonging nowhere, to no one. He was questing for a past. Riding his black stallion, carrying a silver-tipped spear, he crossed streams and sweet meadows, built fires by night, and battled griffins and faceless men. He was lonely and proud in his human trappings. I set him free again, into his wildness of trees and stags, so that he rose like an oak in my mind, sinewy and polished, with his antlers flaming in the setting sun. His eyes were dark as stones. I saw him piecemeal, in my half sleep: a thigh, a breast, a hand. He turned into a tree then. My mind touched its bark, drew down it again and again, until it was soft, muscular, warm with light. The tree trunk split into a hollow of darkness near the roots. My mind touched the darkness, and the Stagman stood free again, a potentially dangerous situation. He had two tongues; they were both three seconds long. There was an oak branch between my legs and warm oak breasts under my hands. I kept my mouth shut. The oak branch shuddered under me, and a holy hermit said, "That is not the light." But I clung to the oak until its shuddering stopped, and I half woke to hear my heartbeat.

"What are you doing?" Frances whispered.

I turned over to stare at the dark ceiling. There was nothing, no lightning bolt, no church toppling on its foundations, no angels choiring in divine dismay. Only something very simple, so simple I wondered for a moment if I was on the same planet. "It's your Stagman," I mumbled sleepily. "It felt good. I don't understand what all the fuss is about." There was a silence. "Frances." I pushed myself up, feeling suddenly lonely in the dark, with an ancient mystery of good and evil no more than a brief flush of sweetness between my legs. "Frances."

"I'm here," she said.

I was watching Justine. She stood on the sidewalk outside the school, talking to her boyfriend. Her skirt was rolled crookedly; her hair was tangled. She gestured with *The Hobbit* in one hand, then laughed at something, and the boy, a thin redhead with a cigarette in his fingers, laughed with her. Sister Anthony came down the steps; he dropped the cigarette to the walk and stepped back onto it in a cool, practiced movement. His smile was quick and light, covering his whole face. I had a brief vision of them French kissing. But they just kissed quickly, like children. Then Justine came into the building, and I stepped back from the window. She came into the classroom, unrolling her skirt and smiling vaguely. I wanted to talk to her suddenly. About what, I wasn't sure. About night dreams, and morning longings, about being able to laugh . . . I sat down at my desk and opened a notebook. The Stagman appeared unexpectedly on its pages, lonely and solitary, in a silent forest of ancient trees. He hesitated, searching for a reason to go in one certain direction. But there was no path, no sign; the trees rose about him, gray, still, sunless. Frances was sitting still in her desk, her head bent a little; she was lost in thought. A ray of light appeared in the forest; the Stagman moved toward it: Justine's voice, raised in one of her arguments over dogma.

"Look." She flipped her history book open at random. "Page after page of it—he, he, he. Look at all those gray faces. Men slaughtering each other, men making peace, men sitting around tables talking about money, weapons, sin . . . I get so sick of that pronoun. He." She glared at the crucifix hanging above Sister Margaret's empty desk. "We worship a pronoun."

"Oh, Justine, shut up," Liz said disgustedly, and Agnes added with an edge to her usually gentle voice, "God is a spirit; He doesn't have anything to do with sex."

"We're supposed to be perfect, even as our heavenly Father is perfect. I'm not physically equipped to identify with a man."

"He means everybody," Debbie argued. "Like mankind. 'All men shall be brothers.' It means women, too."

"Then why don't we say that? All women shall be sisters."

"It's implied," Liz said shortly. She was a straight-A student and a member of the Sodality, so she was equipped to argue religion.

"I'm not a man," Justine said. "I'm not a brother. I'm tired of spending half my life studying about men, putting he's into my head. What if it was the other way around? What if guys had to go through their puberties reading books by women, about women, hearing lectures about women, doing reports about women, taking tests about women, being told they should be perfect even as their Heavenly Mother is perfect, What a piece of work is a woman, how noble in form, how infinite in faculty, Our Mother who art in heaven, a mighty fortress is our Goddess—" She started to grin in spite of herself. Debbie was cracking up.

"They'd all be fruit cakes."

"Fourscore and seven years ago our foremothers declared all women shall be equal."

"The peace of the Lady be with you."

"In the name of the Mother, the Daughter, and the Holy It."

Something terrible was happening in the forest. Trees were crashing all around the Stagman. He couldn't move; massive trunks tore out of the earth, crashed before him, behind him. His horse was dancing in terror, but the trees piled around it; it couldn't run.

"Thou shalt love the Lady thy Goddess with thy whole heart, thy whole soul, thy whole mind, thy whole strength—"

"This is my beloved Daughter, with whom I am well pleased."

"Unto us a Queen is born, unto us a child is given—"

"And the Daughter of Woman shall sit in judgment."

"Mother, into thy hands I commend my spirit—"

"Our hearts shall never rest, O Lady, until they rest in Thee."

There was a short silence as they looked at one another. Even Agnes was smiling a little. For a moment the silence was like the silence after a song; the words of it were comforting, rich with possibilities. Then a sound broke into the silence: the wounded, broken cry of the Stagman. Frances sniffed, and Justine, closing her history book with a bang, turned to her in amazement.

"Frances." Tears were plopping all over her religion homework. "Frances." Justine crouched beside her, touched her, tried to see her face. "What is it? What's wrong?"

But she could only shake her head, trapped in silence,

while within her the Stagman cried her confusion in his voice.

Then two things happened: It started to rain a dreary November rain, and the principal, Sister Mary Alleluia, flicked on the PA system with a noise like an eardrum popping and cleared something out of her throat. "Girls," she said very wearily, not bothering to bid us good morning, and as huge words lumbered into the room—Dallas, sniper, president, death—*The Once and Future King,* with its unicorns, courts, luminous quests, and high destinies, slid off Frances's desk, fell face down on the floor.

"Frances!"

Justine stopped on the church porch as we waited for the rain to die down after school. Even she had lit a candle in the heart of lights in front of the Blessed Virgin—she who had scorned what she had called the Cuban Missile Crisis Catholics. Her eyes were red; her face, like all our faces, looked splotchy and tired. Frances's face was simply frozen; she was shivering a little in the wind. I stood behind her like a shadow.

Justine shrugged a little at the question in Frances's eyes. "I just wanted to wait with you. My boyfriend's coming to pick me up in a few minutes. I don't feel like being alone."

Frances looked vaguely surprised. She wasn't used to the idea that anyone had a choice in the matter. She spoke for the first time since morning. "What's your boyfriend's name?"

"Terry. He goes to Loyola High. Do you have one?"

"What?"

"A boyfriend."

Frances shook her head. Justine sat down on the steps under an angle of roof. She thought a moment, then sighed. "No. They'd kick me out of school for smoking on the church steps." Her eyes filled again suddenly, and she muttered, "Oh, shit." She blew her nose and stared glumly at the rain. "God. I feel so sad. And I'm a Communist."

"You are?"

"Oh, not like the Russians. They're cruel. But think of people living together, in beautiful places, in mountains, beside the sea, in churches, even in museums and parks, just living, being kind to each other, sharing what they create—music, fresh bread, children—just leading simple lives and being happy together—no guns, no bombs, no gray faces in history books declaring war, just people caring for each other. It's possible. It has to be possible. But half the world sits on a pile of gold making bullets, while the other half dies of starvation." She chewed furiously at a fingernail a moment, frowning away tears. Then her attention came back to Frances, standing on the step above her. "Debbie got hysterical at lunchtime; she's such a baby. You're so still. Why were you crying this morning? Did you have a premonition?"

"No." She sat down finally beside Justine. I felt the cold through my sweater and blazer, in my wet hair. The porch step seemed icy under me. Frances wiped rain off her face with her sleeve, then clasped her arms tightly around her knees, hunched over her heart. The Stagman wandered down the street in front of us, drenched, lost, despairing, searching the empty sky for a sign.

"I just felt—I just felt that there was something very wrong."

"A premonition," Justine said. Frances's shoulders slumped. We watched the rain. The street was flooded with water. It was a long road, with voices of wind and sorrow, the Stagman's voice and Frances's voice, he and she, winds in the outside world weaving into an inextricable knot. For a moment, as the world emptied again around us, my thoughts grew gray as the rain, and the roads of the city tangled, running nowhere. My skin turned cold, like the stones of the church or a tower, feeling nothing; there was no path out of my mind. I breathed the Stagman's air; I had no name behind my face. There was only Frances, who had gotten us so tangled up in imagination I could barely keep the world in order anymore. "I knew it," Justine added. "You always look like you're listening to another world."

"I live in this one," Frances said, and I came back to it, breathing again.

Justine looked at her, sitting damp and patient as a mushroom in the rain. She said suddenly, "You're scared, aren't you? I can see it a lot of times in your eyes."

Frances nodded. "I was born scared. It's like not having a skin. Just nerve endings." She added, "I don't know why."

"Christ. How can you live like that?"

"I won't always. Someday I'll be able to laugh."

A car with a red-haired driver in it shot spray as it came to a halt at the curb. Justine rose, still gazing at Frances.

"I'll tell you something," she said. "You're not the only one. We're all scared. All of us. Liz is scared of hell, Agnes is scared of sex, Marsha is scared of failing, Debbie is scared of her mother, the nuns are scared of the world falling apart, nobody knowing what to do—"

"What are you scared of?"

She paused. "Me?" She smiled a little, crookedly. "That I'm just some dumb kid making D's in history, who'll never do anything worthwhile. That's why I wanted to get to know you. I needed to know what you thought of me because you're someone I respect."

She turned, leaving Frances staring at her back. It took her a full minute to move after the car surfed away from the curb. The man with cut shoes wandered into her silence and was caught in her imagination. He tossed an empty bottle in the gutter, sending it swirling down the flood after the Stagman, with or without a message of hope.

5 ~ WASTELAND

The school changed, but the pepper trees didn't. They grew immense, impossibly gnarled, forming knots and boles and twisted roots to hide their inner scarring. They shed knife-thin leaves and berries down the sidewalk from the university library, past the science building to the men's PE building, with its maze of corridors, stairways, and courts that I solved once a semester, following signs and painted arrows, doors, saying "No Entrance," "Left only," and "No Exit" when I registered for classes. The library, where Frances and the Stagman lived, was as complex, but she knew its stairs and stacks and dim, quiet places better than I wanted to. I lost her, somewhere, in front of a door saying "No Exit and No Entrance" or maybe down in the bottom of bookstacks, with concrete walls and no windows, among leather-bound books of early English shire maps, early California mining maps, records of court transactions, legal documents. I didn't know where she was going those days. I could only follow her blindly, hoping and terrified.

The first thing she did, still half-dazed from figuring out the mysteries of class requirements, biology, philosophy, English lit, history books still unbedraggled in her arms, was to get me pulled into a packed current of bodies that snaked its way, chanting. through the placid university grounds. "On strike!" it rumbled. "On strike! On strike!"

"We can't be on strike," I said bewilderedly. "We're in a university. We're supposed to be learning how to think. That's like our brains going on strike."

Arms locked all around me, in solidarity, pulling me forward, and I grabbed at a volume of English poets that an elbow jostled out of my arms. Boys, I found, had changed alarmingly while I hadn't been paying attention. They had acquired whiskers and brains, wire-rimmed glasses that winked with frosty certainty. "Stop the draft!" someone bellowed behind us, and the cry was passed down the line. "Stop the draft! Stop the draft!"

"I have to get to my English class," Frances said desperately, trying to duck under an armpit.

"You don't lay your life on the line, girl, someone will lay it down for you. In a box."

"Huh?"

"I get drafted, I'm going to kill or be killed. I don't want to kill."

Something in the voice dragged her eyes up. The current had flung her against brown, sweating skin, smooth and muscular as oak. The face, above turquoise beads, was midway between greasy french fries and dignity. The eyes were dark, at once hard and gentle. An oak branch flared above his wild hair. "I don't want to kill," he said again, softly.

Frances swallowed. Something stirred in her face beneath its bonelessness, something not quite alive, moving in its blind sleep. Then there was another shout; the line surged forward, its deep voice charged, marching: "ROT-C. ROT-C." We broke through a picket line—teachers or cafeteria workers, I wasn't sure. The ROTC building loomed in front of us. Glass shattered. There were shouts. The line loosened, scattered. I ran with it, ducking between parked cars, through groups of students. I collapsed finally on a bench, in a corner behind the home economics building. Ivy cascaded down the stucco behind us. The wall was warm under my back; it blocked the chaos and shouting. Two professors, chatting amiably, crossed the sunlit grass and pulled open a side door. Above my head, pots rattled; something was burning. I closed my eyes. It didn't matter about the English class, I thought tiredly after a while. Dr. Jameson had been in the picket line. In the sunlit silence I finally heard Frances's voice.

"War," she whispered. Thinking back, I realized how long we had been waiting for it.

Within the stucco buildings in the heart of a gently dilapidated city lay an unbelievable dragon's hoard of images. The Hound of Heaven pursued the Green Knight across a wasteland of no water, only rock; dark, sweet violets grew on pregnant banks, vaster than empires and more slow. The stars had names; light was measured. I played the flute and dissected an unborn pig. Had it been born, it would have spoken wisely in some poem or old myth. Leaves contained a million cells; the day sky acquired depth. Legends roamed across the well-kept grass, drank from the fountain, vanished back into the whale's belly of the library, where they lived in the spaces between neatly ordered lines of print. Collections, anthologies, summaries, translations navigated us relentlessly toward a past; our polar star was a strange, masculine despair. Frances collected messages that blew like tumbleweeds across dry, waterless pages, sometimes to the sound of bullhorns and breaking glass. Her whole attention was focused inward. She was escaping into the Stagman's tale, leaving me to fend for sanity in a world that was rapidly losing its lovely medieval geometry, where once numberless angels had danced on pins and the orbits of planets enveloped the world with layer upon layer of harmonious crystal, breathing soft, singing airs as they turned.

She began to dwindle away. She looked pale, anemic, ineffectual. If a boy spoke to her, she would bump into a door, or trip on a water fountain. Their deep voices, the texture of muscle and whisker, confused her. She walked among them with her head lowered, shielding her body with her books, trying to convince them she was invisible, until she could disappear into the silence and shadows at the bottom floor of the library bookstacks, into the Stagman's safer company. She left me to cope with papers, languages, the analysis of poetry, the occasional, unpredictable voice that threatened to remind her of her own existence.

There was one voice she almost listened to. It was gentle, tenor, humorous. The owner of it, a slight, dark boy in my basic drawing class, brought in beetles, dragonflies, butterflies, and drew them with tiny dots of charcoal, instead of lines, as meticulously as a scientist.

"The world is a circle," he said. "Everything is circular, no endings, no beginings. Except my mustache." He touched the fine hair on his upper lip, that he was nursing patiently into manhood. His smile was like his voice, contained and wry. His beetles fascinated me. Out of the corners of my eyes I watched them grow; I watched him, tinking his pencil on the edge of a jar to make his subject shift. He was happy drawing bugs instead of vases; he joked about his body, which was still growing, dot by dot; about the world, which he said was insane enough to justify his drawings. He sensed me watching him one day. His pencil tinked again, inside a plastic cup. He set the cup beside my elbow, startling me. I looked up into his face for the first time, surprising myself, and then down at the cup.

"What's that?"

"Coffee-wash," he said.

"What?"

"A little *café au lait* and some water." He waved a dry brush like a wand over the dead leaves I was trying to draw. "You can get some delicate shadings with washes. Put more cream in it if it's too dark." He drifted back to his work, while I dabbled coffee over my drawing. The leaves only looked drowned, but when he came back a few moments later to laugh at them, he made me laugh, too. For a moment something heavy, fearful, inside me dissolved. I saw the afternoon sun stretched gold as a saint's halo through the dusty air, and I realized, in that moment, how timidly I always breathed. I took a deeper breath, easing into my own body, and then he said,

"Frances. Can I buy you a hot-dog after class? Or bean-sprouts, whatever it is you feed yourself with? We can talk."

Frances froze. She couldn't talk, and even if she could how could I bring a Stagman from out of all his secret dwellings into the normal air? The name confused me, pulled me into two different worlds at once, one real, one imaginary, neither of which I understood. He waited, the smile in his eyes darkened by a faint perplexity. I gazed up at him, mute, memorizing the bones of his face, and in Frances's mind the face of the Stagman changed briefly, became younger, open. The friendly artist was still waiting, but she couldn't answer him; she could only transform him, dot by dot, into someone whose actions, on flat, lined paper, she could predict.

I looked down finally, and words came. "Maybe not today. Maybe later."

He turned away; I watched his shadow trail across the light. I heard my own stiff voice in my ears, felt the stiffness of my body. I wanted to yell suddenly; I wanted to throw paints, dance on a desk-top, rage at Frances, step out of my motionless body and eat a dozen hot-dogs. But she had a story to write, and when the bell rang, she threw the

coffee-wash down the sink, and burrowed back into the
security of the library.

"Next time," I threatened her. "Next time."

But there was no next time. The beetle-artist was picked
off by a lottery number and never came to class again. I
didn't know where he went—Vietnam, Canada—but the
swiftness and humorlessness of his vanishing appalled me.

"He was only eighteen," I protested to Frances. "He
didn't even have a beard yet, just duck-fluff. He draws beetles, for God's sake. Really nice beetles. They'll take his
pencil away and put a gun in his hands and he'll just die.
Are you listening? I mean, suppose you wanted a war,
would you trust it to some kid who sits around drawing
bugs? Are you listening?"

"Yes," she said. I was silent awhile, feeling her listening.
I was doing homework. My bedroom, with dark pine knots
staring at me from the paneling, seemed too small suddenly.
The night with its wet horned moon seemed too small. I
thought of myself existing, not existing. Drawing butterflies one day, then vanishing. Someone else in my place
drawing butterflies. While I—what? Drifted into eternal
bliss, with a God who was a stranger? Intimations of im-
mortality chilled me. "I haven't begun to feel yet," I whispered numbly. "I haven't begun to feel."

"I'm listening."

"If I don't touch things, I won't die. If I don't speak, I
won't die. If I don't know I'm alive, I won't die. Will I.
It's better not to talk, not to touch. . . ."

She couldn't answer; she had no answers. I got up,
pushed my nose against the window. The glass reflected

inward and outward: the lit room, books scattered on the bed, my dark face; the streetlight weeping down to the ground, spangling rain in the gutter; the dark, blank face of the night. "I don't understand. I don't understand my bones. I don't understand the position of the moon. I don't understand what I want. . . . I could die tomorrow. To-night, if I close my eyes. I'm not even alive yet, and I could die."

"You've been alive for years."

"I know, but this is different. I want, and I don't know what I want, and I'm afraid I'll die before I know what it is, I'm afraid. . . . Nothing helps, not saints or the love of God. This has nothing to do with God. It might have some-thing to do with beetles." I was whispering again, hoping no one, not even myself, would hear. "I don't think God is real, anymore than your Stagman is real. It's just another tale, another protection against the world. Against fear."

Frances was somewhere else, not wanting to hear me, in a less dangerous world. She left me alone to face implica-tions. I picked at paint, crying and not crying, and the moon remained stubbornly the moon, a perplexing chunk of stone, while Frances used it as a beacon to light the Stag-man's way.

The Stagman changed again, as other, less gentle voices battered at Frances's thoughts, in classes charged with bit-terness, cynicism, terror, hopelessness. The Stagman ab-sorbed her emotions, the emotions around her, growing dark and wild again as, studying and searching for some definition of humanity, we were faced constantly with our own inhumanity.

"War," said Dr. Jameson, after he was rehired after being

fired for striking, "according to Hobbes. 'Hereby it is mani-
fest that during the time men live without a common power
to keep them all in awe, they are in that condition which is
called war; and such a war as is of every man against every
man. . . . In such condition there is no place for industry
. . . no account of time; no arts; no letters; no society; and
which is worst of all, continual fear and danger of violent
death; and the life of man, solitary, poor, nasty, brutish, and
short.' "

"There's no war," somebody drawled from the back of
the room. "Nobody declared war. We've got industry, arts,
letters, society, tile bathrooms. There's no war, only a police
action. We're trying to spread democracy and tile bathrooms to the impoverished, nasty, brutish, short people of
the world. Has he got a definition of a police action?"

"Something that happens on somebody else's territory,"
a girl's voice said.

"We're sending our men to their territory and getting
back a shitload of flag-draped coffins," another voice
snapped. "That's police action."

"We haven't got a common power to keep us all in awe,"
the voice drawled again. "We've got a man with a ski-jump
nose who's a magician. Does magic tricks, sleight of hand.
When is a war not a war? If we're not all in awe, does that
mean we're all at war?"

"All," Dr. Jameson said gravely, his eyes deadpanned
behind thick black frames, "implies the entire social body
contracted, as it were, by birth or citizenship to stand in awe
of the governing power."

"Well, I'm not standing around in awe," a weary voice

behind me muttered. "I'm joining a commune in New Mexico."

There were other voices, gentle, uncynical, advocating peace. Peace lay in the angle between the first and second fingers outspread. Its vision was formed and frozen in a searing incongruity: students placing flowers in the maws of guns held by impassive national guardsmen, who, moments later, may or may not have replied with Mace or tear gas or a liberal application of night sticks. Or later, bullets. And yet there was no war. Anyway, their side had more dead bodies.

> On to the ded gois all Estatis,
> Princis, Prelotis, and Potestatis,
> Baith riche and pur of al degre:
> Timor mortis conturbat me.

That voice was grim, dour, and somehow gloomily satisfied, accompanied by a choir of anguished tenor monks. "Timor mortis conturbat me," I whispered, sitting under a chestnut tree outside the science building. Inside were jars of strange floating animal fetuses, glass cases with fragile reassembled skeletons, rows of fossils of things that had never had voices, had made no sound, ever, before they turned to stone. I could sit under the chestnut tree forever and crumble into dust. I stared at dead leaves, feeling myself flow away from myself in tides. I was at a thin edge of nonexistence. I was only skin, paper-thin. My hands didn't belong to me. I was mute as a trilobite. If I spoke, no one would hear me. If anyone spoke to the illusion of me, I couldn't answer. I was invisible; I had no thoughts. I was afraid, I was afraid. I took up too much space. If I moved, I would acknowledge my own existence. If I moved, I would acknowledge my body. If I moved, I would acknowledge time, space, loneliness, and a flame like the fire of a setting sun moving farther and farther away from me, down to the vast, drear edges and naked shingles of the world.

"I am half-sick of shadows," I whispered, and stood up. I walked around the corner to the library, collecting two leaflets on the way: one demanding a total shutdown of the university in protest of U.S. imperialistic policies, the other announcing a noon rally to castigate the powers that were keeping us all unawed. I found the iron bookstack stairs inside the library and went down to the bottom floor. No one was there. I sat down.

"Frances," I whispered, but she wasn't there. Out of the corner of my eye I saw the Stagman's shadow.

It spilled blood-red down the chipped concrete floor; its staghorns groped at my feet. It was too big for the bookshelves, too big for the library, and it was moving. One step would bring it into vision. I watched muscles shift and gather. The horn shadows tangled like net over my feet. I froze, not wanting to see his face, wanting to see his face, watch it rise like a moon, full and bloody, out of the musty, bookish darkness. Then, as the shadow flowed over me, my fascination turned to terror.

"No!" I grabbed things to throw—books, pencils, anything—heaved them into the darkness to stop him. "I don't want to see you—I don't want to see you—" The flotsam of the bottom floor, spilled over from the upper, airy shelves—oversized books, atlases, dictionaries—sprawled in his path, with bent pages and broken spines. They checked his step; his shadow ceased to move, melted into chipped red floor. I sat down again finally, panting, my arms aching. I sensed him at the edge of my vision, waiting. Then I knew I had never stood, never shouted. There were no books on the floor. They were lined, rank and file, on the shelves; they had been there forever. My arms were aching because I had been gripping the desk. I let go of it, slid my hands over my face, beginning to whimper.

"Oh, Christ. I'm nineteen years old, and I'm going barmy. I don't know what's real, I don't know what's real. Frances is driving me crazy; my own name is driving me crazy. . . ." I heard a sound, then, where the shadow had been. I raised my head, frozen again. A student stood looking at me. He wore jeans and a ragged military jacket held together at the collar with a safety pin. His army crew cut had barely started to grow out. One empty sleeve was rolled up, pinned against the stump of his left arm. Under his other arm he held some great medieval volume full of gold leaf, red Latin letters, flat paintings of saints and visionaries against horizons with no perspective. He was very still in the silence. His eyes were dead.

"I know what you mean." His voice, thin, emotionless, drifted away, returned. "You want to share a joint with me? I live just down the street. . . ."

I got up, mumbling something. His voice pursued me up the stairs. "You don't need reality. Reality sucks."

I dragged myself up into the sunlight, feeling numb and tired. The sky above the concrete and stucco buildings was clear blue; a blackbird streaked across it. I went to an old, scholarly tree full of red and gold leaves and leaned against it, my arm around it. Its bark was rough, warm against my tiredness. *A tree,* I thought wearily, *has an instinct to become a tree. Surely people must have instincts to become themselves if they listen hard enough . . . if they try. . . .* I saw him in my mind's eye, the Stagman, Frances's mirror, and I wondered how the ice-bright Stag which the two sisters pursued had turned into something so terrible. Whose fear and anger was it? Frances's? She had never known how to be angry, only afraid. Mine? Was I that angry with her? With myself? With the world? Or was it all the anger I felt around me, refracted into Frances's imagery? The questions spun in my head, bewildering, unanswerable. I heard shouting in the distance. Students in strike formation came marching down the walk, footbeats keeping time with their chanting: *On strike! Stop the bombing! On strike! Stop the bombing! On strike. . . .* We circled the campus and went down First Street, stopping traffic, while businessmen and secretaries watched, gathered at their high glass windows. With arms around me, people shouting fearlessly, warding off a bloody darkness, I didn't have to think again until night.

I had to let her write. That seemed to be the only way I could understand what was in my head. The shifting landscapes the Stagman rode through were colored by the poetry I studied; his hard despair matched the poets' voices. I didn't know where he was going, what I was doing with him, but Frances seemed to sense something, an ending I couldn't see.

"Look at it," she said. "Look."

He was riding through a wasteland. The sky was dead above it except for one last shaft of light that streaked the harsh sun-battered ground.

"That's from Browning," I said. "Childe Roland. The red light."

"Watch the patterns."

I saw it: a vast, parched land just behind my eyes; the last light of the slow setting sun; the vanishing fire that left hollowness and night behind it. My eyes followed the light; the Stagman's head turned, watching it. It touched his eyes. They had no hope, nothing but knowledge. His great horns cast a dead tree's shadow over the cracked earth. There was nowhere to go but forward. All horizons were the same. He had left all known language behind him. There was not even wind, only air that had not moved since the plain died. With the twilight came strange shadows, memories, echoings of nothing. The red horse he rode was blind.

Something glinted in the fading light, burned silver, then red, then gold. Below a haggard face of dry crumbling rock stood a lovely chapel, rising like a dream out of nothing. A dry riverbed twisted before it; stones loomed all around it. A broken fingernail-paring of moon hung above it. The Stagman stopped.

An owl crouched in his horns. Spiders strung bone-white webs from point to point. A great sword hung from his neck, balanced, as he rode, against one naked thigh. A gauntlet, greaves, a rich coat with one sleeve, bits and pieces of human trappings were all he wore. A squirrel skull hung beside the sword. For a long time he looked at the chapel, while the light drained down the riverbed like water. His face was oaken, expressionless. Then all light faded. In the dusk he held his hands to his heart, his head bowed, as if in petition to some memory. Then he guided his horse toward the dream.

The writing ended. I sat cross-legged on my bed, staring at nothing, holding myself. What dream? I thought. What dream? I heard Frances's voice: "You see? The poetry comes alive. Like a message. . . ."

"Where is he going? What's he going to do there?"

"Wait."

Her fingers tightened on her arms. If a spider had touched her, she would have hit the ceiling. Maybe the ceiling would have fallen; maybe she would have screamed instead of whispering.

"You should be out dating boys." I leaned forward, hiding my eyes against one knee, hardly knowing anymore whom or what I was talking to. "You should be learning how to laugh, how to love. Instead of being trapped in the middle of a story, too scared to come out of it. I wish he would die. I wish he would just die. . . ."

From then on the Stagman attached himself to my shadow. He sat three seats behind me in classrooms, with the owl blinking slowly in his horns, the squirrel skull dangling over the rags of his richness. In my mind's eye I could see him behind me, too big, too barbaric for a desk, listening without moving, breathing without sound. He sat among girls in jeans with feathers in their hair, boys with beads on their bare chests, earrings in their left ears. Sometimes, bearing shock waves from the outer world, their eyes would match his eyes. When I walked through the halls, across campus, he would be there in front of me, all his spider webs gleaming against the frosty sky, his feet naked, soundless on the concrete. I saw him in the midst of antiwar rallies, speches by liberal lawyers, radical priests, even in strike lines, looming over everyone, his shadow forked, flaming across angry, desperate faces. I didn't want to think of doing anything about him. After a while I got resigned to him. Until he came too close, and I looked back once to find not my shadow but his.

"God damn it!" I yelled at Frances. "Nobody else has a Stagman—why should I have one? I'm trying to lead a normal, ordinary, mediocre existence!"

"Then go try it. Just try it."

So I stopped writing and went to work, sloshing food off dirty dishes in the cafeteria and, later, selling clothes to teen-agers in a big department store, to the music of the Jefferson Airplane, the Rolling Stones, the Grateful Dead. But dumping dead french fries down the garbage or putting price tags on lacy underpants I couldn't afford, I saw the Stagman in my mind's eye, an unsolvable problem in quest of an answer. I wrote history papers and sold jeans and dreamed of running away to Scotland. Then, one day, trying to study in the library, I could no longer see the pages in front of me.

I lifted my head. It was raining outside. The clouds were dark. The city looked as if it were crumbling under the rain: neon lights, pawn shops, old chipped stucco buildings. A spastic man moved jerkily along the sidewalk. Two women in black, carrying rosaries, entered the church across the street. I tried to read again, but I couldn't see the words. They melted together, making no sense. Gray water pooled in the gutters where the drains were stopped with leaflets protesting the bombing, protesting the government, protesting the way we lived, protesting the way we died. The rain hit sidewalks, streets, parking lots, concrete and tar, everything but earth. People were hunched silently all around me, not talking, not smiling, not touching. They were absorbing words from pages into their minds, which seemed to me suddenly a peculiar occupation, one which might be handled differently on a different planet. I tried it again. But the dark lines made no more sense than the lines in a stone. I felt something unfamiliar rise inside me, a word no one could hear until I howled it, and they came and took me away to a padded cell, for disrupting the silence of the library. Then a thought checked the rising terror, froze me in my seat. The Stagman was gone, and the world was not making any sense without him.

"Frances," I said, but she was gone, too. People looked up. I didn't howl, and my movements were reasonable, so no one came.

I went home quietly, grabbed one of her stories, curled up in a corner of the bedroom, and ripped it into shreds. I tore page after page until I started crying, knowing that what my hands were doing was hopeless, that what I wanted to destroy lay in my own head and there was only one way to do that. I heard my own voice after a while, talking in short, panting sobs. "I can't. I can't. I can't. I can't. I can't stand living like this, I don't want to live like this, I don't want to live—God, what am I going to do? I walk outside, and the air hurts. I hate myself. I can't use the words other people use. I can't even use my bones right. I don't want to live, I don't want to live—I wish I could turn into something, a door, a wall, anything that doesn't

137

feel." My breathing sounded strange, as if I were trying to hold my head up above water. "I could take aspirin. Or cut my wrists—anything to make the world make sense. I don't want to die, but how can I live like this, in two worlds, one always draining into the other one? I want my name, I want my name, I want my name—" I stared down at my wrists, but there seemed to be the width and solidity of a brick between the outer skin and the faint blue veins. "Do you want to die?" I asked myself, and answered myself, whispering, "No, but how can I live?" I was beginning to drown. I didn't know what to do. There was no Stagman, only rain, sliding like snails down the window. I didn't want to die or go mad. Even the strange world I carried like a boulder on my back was preferable to that. My hands, shaking, cold, tried to put the pieces of the story Frances had written back together again. The Stagman. Frances. Me. If I needed us all to live, to find the end to the confusion, then I had to put the pieces back together. In sudden, blind terror I kept finding fragments that didn't match. My voice sounded like an animal whimpering. Then two pieces went together, and somehow I could read again. The words separated, formed meanings in my mind:

". . . And when they all looked up, he was there, in the doorway, with the last sun burning through his horns, and his sword—"

I looked up, terrified again, and he was there, in the room, looming and dangerous, lifting a new-forged sword.

He smashed the light with it, then the window, splintering the gray sky. I put my arms over my head, ducking down. He saw his face in the mirror, haggard, despairing; the sword drove toward it, and bits of mirror sprayed the

room. Lamps cracked against the floor; books, their bindings
slashed, tumbled to the floor. With a wild, rhythmic grace,
he drew drawer after drawer out of the desk, flung them
across the room. Stationery, nails, glue, stamps, campaign
buttons, old programs, pens, paints arched across the room,
showered against the wall. The drawers cracked and fell to
the floor. The sword wheeled a circle, knocked paintings
off the walls, tore open a pillow. Feathers drifted over us
like snow. His sword lifted once again over my head, and I
shut my eyes and reached for a pen, to draw him back out
of his madness, into the tale we all were trapped in.

A wind wailed across the wasteland. In the dead of the
night no star shone; the sky was black as stone. The Stagman stumbled through the keening darkness that was full
of the voices of dying children, wildcats, bickering women,
toads, men's voices whispering betrayal, gunshots, the
slurred, drunken sibilance of fire. The ground was shaking.
Riverbeds cracked open. Dead weeds caught at his footsteps. Boulders rumbled and crashed around him. In the
dark beyond his vision something was building: a cry without words, a nightmare without a face. The wind's fingers
at his backbone pushed him toward it. The earth shuddered, and shuddered again. Then it split apart, and out
of the opening into nothingness rose a blackness thicker
than night, enormous and cold, towering into the sky. The
wind stopped. The Stagman stood still, ringed with night,
gazing at the ring of stones in front of him. He reached out
finally, found no seam, no door, no passage, only a question
so old there was no language for it.

The pen dropped out of my hand. I leaned back against
the wall, exhausted. My breathing was quieter; the tears

were drying on my face. The vision had gone. The mirror was intact. There was only one feather out of place in the room, lying at my feet in the carpet. I picked it up. My hand shook; I balled the feather in my fist and dropped my face against my knees.

"Christ." I knew then how much I needed her still, how much I needed our separateness, but not her annihilation, how much I feared admitting my own unique existence. To accept being alive was to accept death, and there was no reward of heaven for that, only of the world. She was silent. I had only to say her name and she would be there. I wondered wearily how long it would take me to possess my own name. Then words she rarely used, she didn't know yet how to use—love, passion, experience, laughter—drifted into my head, rich words, unexplored realms that lured me back into a promise of living. Patiently I began to piece together the random, broken sentences on the floor, so that one of us, or all of us, could complete the tale.

The image froze in my mind: the Stagman motionless, faced with the dark tower. He was no longer at my side, in my shadow; his journey had come to a halt. The university itself had nearly ground to a halt then. I sat in a packed auditorium listening to the first tense, ominous phrases of *Finlandia,* while slides of children, hungry, wounded, bewildered, flicked endlessly on a screen placed in front of a burning torch. Few classes met; the administration was trapped in its own ivory tower, alternately bullying and placating until bodies blocking the doors were dragged away. The Student Union was littered with memos, placards, typewriters, leaflets, announcements for meetings of this and that, students playing flutes, holding candles, col-

lecting change for aid, making armbands and posters, pre-
paring bitter petitions to DOW, Lockheed, the governor,
the university trustees who were going to flunk us all, the
president. Through this chaos I wandered, picking up a
poster here, listening to a speech, typing a petition. In my
spare time I stared at the problem in my mind. Different
solutions Frances found with her pen, drawing the story
one way and then another, ended nowhere. The Stagman
stood motionless before the dark tower, through pleas from
the president and quiet candlelight processions for the
dead.

"Mine, O thou lord of life, send my roots rain," the poets
mourned in the pages of my textbooks, loosing falcons of
faith and pleading for sieges and battering rams from
heaven against their despair. Listening to them, to the
desperate voices in the university, considering the great,
looming question that had frozen the Stagman in his path,
I wondered wearily if life might make more sense to
me, lose its cumbersome, historical burden of masculine
despair, if I simply filled my head with a different pronoun.

Behind that thought lay an impossible tangle of gods,
education, stagmen, and Frances. I couldn't think about
them. I studied listlessly so that I wouldn't think, until one
day when I was poring over Milton, listening to him drone,
my mind bumped into a single phrase. I stared at it, shut
my book.

"I quit."

That was that. I lugged my books under my arm, got up
from the bench I was sitting on, and walked into the spring.

"What are you doing?" Frances asked, from out of one of
her hermit's caves in my brain.

"Go away. You and your tower. I'm leaving." I drew breath, feeling clear, sunlit air in my mind.

"You can't just quit!"

"Yes, I can. I'm dropping out. Good-bye. I'll send you a postcard from Scotland." She clung to me like a shadow. "I'm sick of thinking." I breathed again, listening to the amazing, tenuous peace in my mind. "Why didn't I do this years ago? . . . Will you go? Go back into your dungeons."

"Your hands are shaking. You're about to cry."

"Shut up. I'm fine."

"You don't have any money—"

"I'll work." I reached the convertible I used for school and work that belonged to my mother. But instead of going to work, I swung onto a side street and then onto a freeway, going north, since Scotland wasn't south. She was with me, but I didn't have to talk to her.

"You're crying," she said.

"I am not either." I turned on the windshield wipers, then turned them off again. "I wish you would leave me alone. If it hadn't been for you and your crazy stories, I could have been a kindergarten teacher. Or married. Or—"

"You're speeding."

"Since when is seventy speeding? Eighty is speeding, or ninety—" I curved above the city on a ramp, then down again into the hills. It was late, near sunset; the snarls of traffic had dispersed. Shadows cast by the hills flung us alternately into sunlight and night. The big car handled easily, responding with its power steering almost to a wish.

"Buckle your seat belt," Frances said.

"I'm not planning on hitting anything—" But I grappled with the ends until they latched. "Look. I'm not taking you with me. I'm finished. I never want to see that Stagman again, I don't care how his story ends, I don't care, I don't care, I don't care—" There was suddenly a singular absence of Stagman. "Where is he anyway?"

Frances didn't answer. I honed a curve into pure sunlight, wishing I could jettison her out the ceiling with a button. The car dipped, ran again into deep shadow, dark and harsh as the infinite rising of the tower. And there he was, the Stagman, huge, oak-horned, burning with last light, looming up out of nowhere in the middle of my path.

Something shook the car like a wind. I clutched at the wheel as the car decided to make a U-turn in the middle of the freeway. *Follow the skid,* my mind said, *don't hit the brakes.* Or was it, guide the car gently out of the skid? Or was that for ice on the road? My body was jostled in various positions, reminding me of saucering down a snow-covered hill, bumping, blinded, going faster and faster, beginning to lose control, feeling snow on my face, hitting bottom and rolling, gasping, not knowing where my bones would be, yet knowing somehow they would be all there, and all safe. Then I heard glass smash. The car came up, hit me lightly in the face, and stopped.

"Jesus," said the businessman from Saratoga who pulled me out. "I saw that car go out of control—I knew it was going to smash. I just watched it; there's nothing else to do. If you hadn't angled over against the bank before you rolled, you'd have killed yourself. You don't just turn over a convertible and walk away alive. Are you all right?"

"I don't know. Am I?" I was crying in one eye and blind

in the other. A patrolman from Palo Alto was wiping my eye clean. "Am I blind?"

"We'll see in a moment," he said. "Just a moment. What happened? Failure to negotiate a curve?"

No, I'm crazy, my mouth was going to say, there was an oak tree in the middle of the road, but the businessman interrupted.

"Blowout. Look at that back tire. Bald as a baby."

"What?" My eye could blink, if nothing else.

"You had a flat tire," the patrolman said. "That right rear was real bad. I might have to cite you for that." He was smiling a little in relief. "Can you see me? Cut's over your eye, not in it. Eye looks fine."

"I just totaled my mother's car, and you're going to give me a ticket for a flat tire?"

"How fast were you going?"

"Sixty," I lied. He wiped at my eye one last time with his handkerchief.

"Come on. I'll drive you to Stanford. You'll need stitches in that. You can call your parents from there."

I turned to the patrol car. Then I felt the wind again that had shaken the car. It blurred through my mind, and I realized that death was not a dark tower, not even an act of God, but something as impersonal, arbitrary, and ungainly as a hole in a tire. Across the freeway I saw green meadows and fields of oak, lovely and twisted in the last light, and, beyond them, the serene campanile of Stanford, a slender tower rising up over the oak.

I whimpered a little, realizing how close I had come to never seeing oak trees again or fields misted with gold in the sunset. I would never have known how the story ended.

The world seemed very simple in that moment, a matter of light, quiet human voices, still oak.

"It's all right," the businessman said, patting my shoulder. "It's all right. You're alive." But I couldn't stop crying over the chaos and simplicity of it, wondering which story was which, while the slow sun withdrew behind the hills, and all around me, in the living fields, the oak trees dreamed.

"'He for God only; she for God in him.'" It was another week, other voices, women's voices. "Dr. Jameson, I really feel that Milton's attitude toward women was ridiculous and chauvinistic."

"He was a narrow-minded, humorless man," Dr. Jameson said. "God got short shrift in *Paradise Lost,* too. Oddly enough, for a deeply religious man, Milton identified most easily with Lucifer. Chauvinistic. That seems to be the new word for this semester. Why," he asked at a tangent, getting us back on the subject, "does Milton ring his mighty cadences for the devil? What fascinates him so about the horned angel whose name was light?"

"Passion."

The word jumped into the air so quickly I almost glanced around, wondering which of them had said it. But there was only me.

"Very good, Frances."

He looked surprised, too. His eyes wanted me to go on.

My heart was pounding. I had answered to my name. There were no other voices. There was only mine, in a stillness. I could hear it. It kept talking, softly, coherently.

I kept talking. My hands were on the desk in the sunlight. My head was bowed because I was a young woman, a human being too shy to look at anyone. But there were things I had to say, things I knew, things I felt, as a hand feels, closing over a rock or touching the ground, for the first time in its amazing, precarious existence, and this was the beginning of them.

6 ～ LAND'S END

I sat beside a campfire outside a tiny port town in Washington. It was dark. There was only the fire and my hand reaching out to feed it. I was alone. I had driven as far north along the coast as I could without crossing the sound into Canada. That would come later. There were trees all around me; I couldn't see them, but I could sense their stillness. The fire made me remember the sunset, all golds and red-golds fading into tender shades of blue, deeper and deeper into a violet twilight. I thought of portents. I had seen ravens, a small red boat with black sails at noon, and, earlier, an old sailing ship drifting like a dream out of the rising morning mists into blue water and light.

I heard a rustling in the trees behind me. A squirrel, I thought, a raccoon. A bird waking from a tiny bird nightmare. A shift of cloud over the moon darkened its dreams like a hawk shadow. There was no wind. I chipped at a Pres-to-log and put pieces on the fire. I had forgotten an ax, so I had to use a stone. Chopping a Pres-to-log with a stone. *I'm a child of my times,* I thought. *Frances, you are a child of your times.* There were legends in the ground all around me, of bears and wolves and ravens, especially of ravens, but I didn't know them. I remembered my first glimpse of Mount Rainier. Driving along toward a flat horizon under a gray, alien sky, into an older world, I glanced sideways, and it smacked at my vision: an enormous cone looming out of nowhere, raising its head like a great white god, eyeing the world blindly for a few moments before it sank back down out of eyesight. Mountains, water, the northern imminence of space. I thought, *I don't belong here. What am I doing here?* I had followed a road until it would take me no farther. I didn't know where I was going. I didn't understand where I had come from.

I sipped scotch. *I don't understand this planet,* I thought. *Washington trees speak of a different silence. I can't disappear here. People keep bringing me back.* I thought of the woman from Tacoma who brought me a cup of coffee after I put up my pup tent, a small mushroom in a lumbering herd of RV's. The strong wind had torn a loop out; I had to fix it with a safety pin; I had to pound tent pegs with a stone. . . . "You have so much courage," she said, traveling all by yourself, my goodness." I didn't feel courageous; I felt silly. The wind from the sound whipped at my tent all night. Tonight there was no wind, only my fire, and good scotch, and roads that went nowhere.

I drank until the moon set and the water lay dark and still under the mists. Until I forgot how long the road was behind me and how enormous the strange world around me. Until images came, and I could weave them into tales, bright, fragmentary, without hating myself, my weaving, the tales, the scotch, Frances, who was the most incredible coward, who had tried to disappear into her own imaginings. The fire flared when I broke the glass in it. *Tomorrow, I thought, I'll go farther north. Where there will be no tales. Or only tales.*

But I didn't leave, the next day or the day after that. In the morning I sat on the cliff's edge, watching the ferry cross the sound to Victoria. *I'll take the next one,* I thought. The next one. Across the water was a land without memory, without pain. The ferry moved so lightly on the water, dreamlike, stately, elegant. I would step on the next one, let it carry me away to the mist of green and gray that lay along the horizon. I would leave Frances here like a shadow and enter a foreign country. On the guardrail behind me a raven chuckled. *I know,* I answered it silently, crossly. *I am Frances. I've already spent most of a lifetime trying to run away from myself, and it didn't work. So why should this work? I keep running into myself.* In the evening I came back with more scotch. I watched the sun immerse itself like a phoenix in fiery oblivion. I watched the moonrise, stars slowly form their ancient patterns. I wondered, detachedly, why I hated myself so. Because I was half-human. A storyteller, living in imaginary worlds. Because I could hear trees grow and ravens talk, but I was too cowardly to bear the impact of another person's thoughts, another person's feelings. I could feel for myself, for imaginary people, but not for real people. Their emotions, sharp and unexpected as weather, drove me back into myself, like a small bird before a windstorm. I had never learned a language I could share. I had received a degree declaring me a survivor of poetry. I had sold Frances's story of the Stagman. I had trapped myself into writing for a living since I was too frightened to do anything else. I had trapped myself into silence, into my own imagination.

I drank out of the bottle, settled more comfortably against the cliff. *Catch-22,* I thought. A ferry blew a warning blast from its dock, a bellow of hope. I would leave all the confusion here, become the stranger in a strange land. Anonymous, unknown. I would find a new mind, a new face. Frances. The young woman without a past. Maybe I would keep wandering north. Into places of incredible beauty, with little language. Where glaciers ranged across the earth, melted slowly into deep blue water. Where icy mountains, not emotions, dominated. North to the top of the planet, where the sun, shaking color across the night sky, made the only sound, too loud to be heard.

Pine needles crackled; there was a thud beside me, a body sliding into place against the cliff. I turned out of my dream, too drunk to be startled. A young camp ranger, in a green denim suit and hat, had settled beside me. He looked at the dark water far below us, then at me.

"It's a little dangerous here," he commented. His face was

shadowed against the stars, but I knew what it looked like: lean, pale-eyed, humorless. I had seen him without seeing him, emptying garbage, cleaning the bathrooms. His voice was clear, honed with intelligence. He leaned forward suddenly, catching the moon glint on the bottle. He whistled. "This is a hell of a place to get drunk. There are rocks under that tide down there."

"I know." I could feel him looking at me, though I couldn't see his eyes or his expression.

He asked slowly, "What are you doing here camping all by yourself?"

"I'm on my way to Canada." My own voice sounded strange from disuse, high, uncertain. I felt myself becoming defined in his presence, human again, awkward. A young woman alone on a cliff at the land's end, getting drunk by herself in the night. When there were a thousand more interesting, profitable, and civilized things she could be doing. I felt silly and trespassed upon. I wished he would go away. But he took his hat off after a moment, leaned back to watch the stars.

"There's the Pleiades," he said, pointing to a little swarm of diamonds. His finger arced across the sky. "The Hunter."

"Where?"

He traced the stars patiently until I saw the shoulders, the sandal, the sword. His finger moved again. "The North Star. What are you going to do in Canada?"

"I don't know."

"Where are you from?"

I told him. He grunted, eased the bottle from my hand and took a sip. He said, "I used to live down there, in the Bay Area. I had to get away. I couldn't stand the people."

"You like trees better."

"Trees, stars, animals. What do you do for a living?"

"I write," I said shortly. I sensed his sudden attention, palpable as a touch.

"You do?" He added, "I write poetry, in off hours. I live in a trailer, just out of town, in the woods. Sit outside in the evenings, watch the deer and raccoons, sometimes a bear. Sometimes a poem comes. . . . I couldn't do that in a city. You like traveling alone?"

"Sometimes."

"You sound like me. You like solitary places, you can't live with people. A loner. Sometimes I think that's what we're meant to be naturally. But other people's needs screw us up."

I looked down at him. A loner. No need for people. *Is that what I am?* I thought. I took a gulp of scotch. *Christ. I'm this way by nature. There's no hope of change.* The thought should have made me peaceful, but it depressed me. *What kind of writer can I be if I can't stand people?* That thought confused me. Since I couldn't stand writing anyway, why should I care? I drank more, to clear my head. He took the bottle away from me again.

"Take it easy with that stuff. What are you trying to run away from? A bad love affair?"

I shook my head. Hardly. "Just . . ." I shrugged. A terrible thing was happening in my throat; my voice was getting scratchy. "I just can't—" My eyes were filling up; so was my nose. *It's the scotch,* I thought dimly. *I don't even feel like crying. What's there to cry for?*

"Hey—" His fingers found my wrist, circled it. "Take it

152

easy. Whatever it was, you're safe from it here. What's your name anyway?"

"Frances."

"You have friends in Canada? A place to stay?"

"No."

"You're just going."

"Yes. Tomorrow. On the next ferry."

He was silent, his fingers around my wrist lightly, a bracelet, a handcuff. I was suddenly too shy to try to see his face. I heard his breath stop, then start, then stop again.

"Why don't you stay here for a while? I have a friend who needs someone to take care of his house for a couple of months. You could write there. I could show you my poems. It's a beautiful place to write, here. It'd be nice for me to have someone to talk to. Someone like me."

My head cleared for a moment; my body was restless, uneasy, wanting to shift away from his gentle hold. But there was no place to go, and he was probably right. *Why not?* I thought. *Why not? A house to work in, beautiful country, a friend to talk to, probably make love to.* His thumb was moving slightly, tracing veins in my wrist. It felt callused, a good, work-hardened hand. I saw it chopping wood, feeding raccoons. This is how things happen. You sit in the dark and a stranger drops into your life unexpectedly and defines you. He was talking again.

"You seem pretty quiet, peaceful for a woman. I mean underneath all that drinking. Self-reliant, too. I watched you pounding in tent pegs with a rock. I used to have a girl friend in Seattle. We liked each other a lot, but she was all feelings, all emotions. She lived out here with me a few weeks, but she couldn't take the solitude. I kept trying to tell her that she could be happy anywhere if she'd just let herself be, that deer can be as interesting as people, and a lot easier to live with. But she said she needed people, so she went back to the city. She said I didn't understand her, but I think she didn't understand herself. She needs other people to tell her what she is. You are what you are; you don't need other people to tell you that."

I stopped breathing. The stars and moon had disappeared; I was enveloped in darkness, listening to the storyteller's voice in the tide. *Only one sister returned to the house in the forest after the stag hunt. And no one knew which sister it was because she never left her house again, and even she didn't know—*

"What?"

I hadn't realized I'd made a sound. The stars came back; his hand brushed across them, touched my face. "Are you crying again?"

"No."

He sat up, a shadow against the stars. My breath stopped again; my mind fragmented like a kaleidoscope into images: raccoons, stars, trees, ships, a house I hadn't seen, a woman I didn't know. The sound and the sky stretched endlessly into space, into nothingness. A strange man's lips touched my cheek, found my mouth. He smelled of damp ground and trees; there was no dishonesty in his voice. He asked for simple things. He offered me all I was looking for. "Frances," he whispered, and I didn't know whom he was naming, a woman he had defined or a woman he had invented in the dark. I only knew that I was suddenly,

intensely jealous of a woman I'd never met, who needed
to feel, who needed people.

I stood up so fast I nearly fell off the cliff. The scotch
bottle sailed into space; his hold on my wrist broke. He said
something, but I had already climbed under the guardrail.
You're always running, I thought contemptuously, as I ran.
Small roads glinted under me, still gray waterways winding
among the trees, leading me back. Always. There were no
footsteps behind me. My mind was blank for a long time
after I burrowed into the tent. I wished I hadn't thrown
the scotch away. After a long time I fell asleep.

I saw him the next morning, driving the ranger pickup,
as I packed the tent in the car trunk. His face was lowered
under his hat; it looked quiet, indrawn. He didn't look at
me as he passed. I watched the back of the truck, not
knowing why I had stopped moving. Then a new thought,
like a hatchling, broke open in my brain. I thought: *Frances,
you dodo.* I was as insensitive as a fence post, so used to myself hurting it scarcely occurred to me that I could hurt
someone else. He had already had one woman run away
from him. . . . He was emptying garbage when I came
up to him. He nodded coldly, a little surprised, but didn't
speak. So I spoke.

"I'm sorry. I was just—a little drunk and upset. I didn't
mean to hurt your feelings."

His face loosened a little, surprised again, but at something in himself. Then he smiled. It was a true smile,
lighting his eyes, and it made me smile back. I had made
him dislike himself, then like himself again. It was a curious, unexpected power.

"It's all right. I figured you were a little shy." He glanced back at my campsite. "You missed the morning ferry."

"I know. I heard it leave without me."

His eyes came back to me; he hesitated a moment, then added, "A psychologist I read says that shyness is hostility."

I thought: *Shyness is pain, torment, a handicap, a thousand hells of fear of asking for the simplest of needs.* But the idea was a protection to him, made him feel better. I had put the smile back on his face, and I wanted to keep it there. So I just said, "Maybe," accepting the blame. *Maybe he's right,* I thought as I turned. *About everything. I'm rejecting a lover and a house in the woods. And for what? For what? For an instinct, a feeling. Maybe I'm only running again, running again from what I need most. Or maybe I'm going home.*

Home. The vast northern frontier with its singing foghorns and dark winds blowing out of wildernesses of earth and water had made me small, uneasy. I had no patterns of living in it. I drove through twilight, far into the night to get away from it, until I began drifting into half dreams at the wheel. I found a vacancy sign finally, with an upside-down *V.* I rang the night bell and watched an old man in pajamas creak and sigh into the light. It was a still, shriveled hour; the moon looked meager, and the cold air sweated. I got a key to an empty room, a toilet seat with a ribbon around it, a bar of soap too small for anyone over the medieval age of reason. I crawled between chilly sheets and put a quarter in the vibrator. The bed, murmuring of highways and engine throbs, took me into its arms and shook me to sleep.

The next morning I lay staring at a bloated green ceramic lamp beside an empty mirror and wondered what in God's name I was doing there. A moment later I wondered why I felt I should be anywhere else. I closed my eyes, and the room disappeared.

I was in a forest, somewhere between waking and sleeping. Someone was telling a story. "Once upon a time . . ." Maybe it was me, talking to myself as I moved through the cold mists among the trees. I had lost something or forgotten something—a thread of the story, some part was missing. "There were boars," I whispered. "There were towers and Hell-Giants. Castles, stags, nuns." I sifted dead leaves, peered myopically through the mists, naming, enumerating. "What's missing? It's a good story, why am I still looking? What am I looking for, why am I not finished?" I counted my hands, then my eyes. "What is it?"

Something crashed through the mists near me: a dead branch, a boar. I stopped. It was neither of those things. I waited, aware of the tiny, opaque beads of water on tree bark, the way the still grass curved silently toward the sound. The mists seemed to freeze among the dark branches, glittering faintly, like angels' hair. I stopped breathing. Someone breathed within the mists, just beyond my sight. For a moment I thought it might be human. Then the quality of it changed, quickened, softened; the mists swirled, diaphanous as scarves, and I heard my own breathing in my half sleep and opened my eyes to see the mirror flooded with light.

The clouds through the bathroom window shifted across

the sun, and the mirror went blank. My throat made a noise of confusion, longing, desire for coffee. I sat up, swung my feet to the rug. "I want to go home," I said. "I don't have a home. Oh, Christ, a woman with nice anklebones shouldn't have to be sitting in an empty hotel room after having crossed unfamiliar land. What is it I want? What is it? Why have I chosen to be nowhere? What is it my heart can see?"

I drove that day through the lush, silent rain forests that had grown over hundreds or thousands of years near the coast. Indians still lived in them on the farthest strip of western land, on the heavy, brooding coast. Towns were few and small; the people I spoke to were invariably friendly. Their voices were slower than I was used to, as if the state existed in a different time zone, one with longer seconds for shaping words or holding pauses. I drove quickly, drawn south, my whole heart pulled south, an instinct in my blood like migration, that now was the time to be driving south on that lonely highway, though I didn't know why. The road drew inland, crossed farmland and logging camps. I bought a hamburger, ate it on the bank of a silty green river, so slow and opaque it barely reflected the gray sky or the singing reeds. Later in the afternoon the quality of light shifted. The sun came out, illumining a burned forest, so that each tree bone, each gray, dry trunk, worn to driftwood by the seasons, seemed to burn again from within. In that stretch of light, after seven hours of driving, I entered the strange, dazed mood I was familiar with: of traveling forever toward evening, which would never come, so I would never stop, and the sweet, mystical late-afternoon light would never change, I would

158

be traveling in it forever, which wouldn't matter because the world beyond it had ceased to exist. But it changed; the sky grew shadowed again, and I saw water. Then I saw the great bridge between the frontier of Washington and Astoria.

It passed straight over the water, then rose gradually to an immense dark angle midair above the trawlers and barges in the bay beneath. It was a portent, like the moon or Mount Rainier, binding two lands, bringing the traveler out of wild forests to face the open sea, to taste brine and watch the evening sun color the waves like abalone before it set. *Here,* I thought, watching lovely old Victorian houses set in the hillsides of the city lit for evening, *is another place I don't have a bed in.* Driving farther down the coast, past the small towns near the sea that were painted in pastels and sandy tones, worn by the wind, I searched for a place to rest. But all the doors seemed shut, all the windows turned away from me, facing the sea. *I'm tired,* I thought. *So tired.* In the distance something gleamed: a ship crossing the horizon, reflecting invisible light. The great eye of a lighthouse on a jut of land slid across the twilight, searched me in an instant, then turned away. It left its eye in my heart, though: a moment of warmth, a blink of illumination. Then something crossed the road just beyond my headlights. I braked, and it flowed silently back into the shadows. I braked harder, half recognizing it; a truck behind me tooted impatiently. Around a coil and dip of road, something dark reared its head into my vision. A stone as big as a cathedral, with a cluster of lights around it. I thought of holy exorcisms, and I drove toward the incoming tide.

The lights were a tiny town that had grown up facing the rock. It stood just beyond the tideline, with a fretwork of foam at its base. Rock worshipers came every summer to look at it apparently, for half the town was cottages and motels. I drove past the motels and onto the beach to gaze at it, wondering how a hoary battered rock shaped like a haystack with a crown of grass and a halo of sea gulls around it could make me feel peaceful. It was rooted, I decided finally, and it housed living things. I found a bed in one of the motels, where I could dream of stones at night and listen to the sea.

Morning drew me out, down the road, across the sand to stare at the rock. I saw its priest standing at the base in a Windbreaker and jeans, exhorting his congregation. His body and outstretched arms made the shadow of a long cross down the sand. The tide had drawn back to reveal the life clinging to the sides of the rock: huge starfish and fist-sized anemones with delicate pink and green tentacles, mussels, barnacles, little scuttling crabs, sea mosses, and seaweed like miniature palm trees. A group of school kids ran past me toward the priest. I heard his voice faintly above the gulls' voices: "Careful, don't slip. Don't go past the warning signs, it's dangerous. Okay, kids, I want you to gather around this tidepool. . . ." Behind him, the mists grew pink and oyster gray as they loosed the sun. The waves roared exuberantly, and the sea gulls gabbled a hymn to the great, weary rock.

I stayed there all day, wandering up and down the single street, eating supper on the beach. I watched the tide circle the rock once more, hiding the sea villages around it. The sun set into mists; the rock grew shadowed, hunched. I felt its stillness seep into my bones, felt rooted in the sand, heavy and tired, motionless. The gulls would nest in my hair; the barnacles cling to my ankles. I would sit there forever at the tide's edge, letting the sea and wind shape me, harden me, loving a rock because I had nothing else to love. The sea would be my home; the rock's strength, my strength. I huddled against the dusk wind, wondering what tale I could possibly tell myself that might change the way I looked at the world. I was used to silence; I could let the winds blow through me, emptying me of all thought. There was nothing else worth doing, no place else worth going. I stared into the twilight, searching for the candle ends of old tales, but nothing sparked in me, drenched the quiet coming night with fire. The wind grew dark; I heard the tide take on its hollow evening voice. Something I hadn't noticed formed at the tide's edge. My eyes picked out shape from shadows. Someone stood there silently: another rock worshiper, another pagan drawn by suns and stones and tides. Whoever it was moved as I watched, came slowly toward me, past me, steps making no noise above the tide. I turned away from the rock, still watching, acknowledging my own bones and blood in the movement, that I was not wind, I was not a stone. The full moon was rising over the forest beyond the town. The great pale eye seemed to rest for a moment in the leafless branches of a tree, but the tree moved as the moon lifted, and they weren't tree boughs the moon was tangled in, but the ancient, oaken horns of the stag.

"You," I whispered. "You."

I saw his body, silvered with light, just as he faded. He had brought me to my feet. I stood shivering, no longer part of the evening, thrown up on the shores of the living, responsible to my own body. "Who are you? What are you that won't die?" Nothing answered me. I started walking, needing a place to go, having no place to go, and I sensed him behind me, driving me, ahead of me, marking my path, a mystery.

I heard music as I left the beach, from a bar on the main street. I stopped in front of its door, stood listening. The door was of dark wood, with a stained-glass window of a mermaid hoisting a mug of beer with one hand and holding a trident with the other. Behind her were the sea and the rock, with the sun rising over her left shoulder. Her long yellow hair fell over her naked breasts; she grinned cheerfully, winking at the world, inviting it in. The music was rocking the walls around her. It beat at my silence; all I could do in there would be to search for sandy stag prints. I felt myself dwindle into my own body, with windblown hair and small, vague face. I opened the door, got a confused image of pool tables at one end of the place and a rock band at the other, people dancing, loggers or fishermen in cowboy hats playing pool, a young dark-eyed bartender giving me the same wink and grin that the mermaid did before he turned to set a foaming mug of draft down in front of the Stagman.

I found the darkest corner of the room and ordered wine. A stag's head above the pool table gave me a glassy, haunted gaze. Cold and tired, I sipped wine, watching girls in long cotton skirts, in jeans and cowboy boots. They seemed part of a different world; I wished I could dance to their music, smile their smiles. A small freckled waitress set a second glass of wine down in front of me. "From the man at the bar," she said. "The dark one. He said to ask if he could join you." Her expression seemed a little bewildered, as though she had seen something but didn't want to believe it.

"I don't care," I said.

"He said yes or no."

"Huh?"

"He wanted you to say yes or no. That's what he said."

I looked at her. There seemed no reason to answer, but he had brought me in out of the cold. So I said, "Yes," which was as easy as saying no. The waitress nodded and left. But no one joined me. After a while I glanced toward the bar. He was sipping beer, looking primitive and mildly absurd, stark naked on a barstool, with an owl sleeping in his horns. But no one seemed to notice. The bartender tossed him a casual word now and then; he answered. I watched the muscles flow along his skin as he drank. His skin was a dark, rich gold all over, even where the hard muscles of his buttocks broke their lines against the leather of the barstool. I could see only part of his face: a high, flat cheekbone, a jawline, dark lashes, a line beside his mouth. I wondered what he was paying for the beer with. I finished my own wine and began the glass he had bought me. The colors in the room seemed brighter, slightly misty; every face in the room seemed to be enjoying its own existence. One of my feet began tapping to the music; I watched the Stagman idly, wondering where he'd been since I ran into him with the convertible. I hadn't felt the lack of him, but he did insert a question into the world, sitting there, like the soundless vibration the string bass was sending through the floorboards. Something I couldn't ignore. I wondered where he'd been. He shifted a little, loosening his hand and bringing his forefinger gently down on the bar to make a point. His hands were big, gold-brown, the fingers beautifully, evenly jointed. I glanced around suddenly, wondering if any other woman in the room could see him. *He's mine,* I thought, *he belongs to me. I invented him.* I was jealous suddenly; whether I wanted him or not, I didn't want anyone else to have him. His shoulder blades gleamed in the soft bar light. I fidgeted, watching women's faces as they passed him. They didn't seem to notice him, but how was I to know if he might suddenly become obvious, some golden, primitive idol in a land full of weather-beaten loggers. A girl with fine silver-blond hair down to her waist came toward him, and I got up. She walked past him without a glance, but I was already up. So I took my wineglass to the bar and edged onto the stool next to him.

For a while I couldn't speak. I just drank wine and felt him next to me, someone of me but not of me. Letting my eyes flicker up now and then, I could glimpse his face and the great horns in the mirror among the scotch bottles. His eyes were hidden. The bartender put a third glass of wine in front of me. I traced the rim of it a few times, then took a sip. His knee was very close to mine, but not touching; his forearm as he lifted beer nearly brushed mine but never touched. I felt him rather than looked at him; a thousand questions wove, in stillness and small movements, between our bodies.

I said finally, "I thought I killed you."

He turned his face then, and I met his eyes. I felt myself vanish, then turn into stone. The bar disappeared; the sea disappeared. I saw him again; without moving, he touched me everywhere, pulling me like gravity, like tide. He was an upright stone straining toward the moon, a vampire, a kelpie, a knight in shining armor, a resurrected god. I saw the muscles of his breasts, his mouth, his thighs. I felt my body flow toward him without moving. I felt as if I had circled the world in a breath, and my hands were still crooked around my wineglass.

What are you? The question came from deep within my mind, in a voice I had never used before. He didn't answer; he simply faded away, a mystery, a desire, a warning, leaving me changed, unfamiliar to myself, not knowing any longer which of us had been the pursuer and which the pursued.

7 ⤙ STAGMAN

Suddenly wherever I looked there were stagmen. On sidewalks, in gas stations, rising on escalators, disappearing behind closing elevator doors, on top of telephone poles fixing lines, driving trucks, poised with pencil in hand to take my hamburger order. Smiling or unsmiling, with bald heads, flaccid bellies, brown hands with a hard tracery of tendon and vein, dirty nails, clean, buffed nails, muscled forearms with faint lines of blue at the crook of the elbow, where the rolled sleeve fabric ended and, in shadow, the naked skin began.

Feet. They walked across the pages of my writing. Big, splayed, calloused feet, long, tanned bony feet, saints' feet out of Renaissance paintings, elongated, mutely expressive. My father's feet. Christ's anguished feet. Pale feet, like hothouse plants, that shied away from the sun. Wild feet, brown all over, that pounded after Frisbees in the surf. The Stagman's feet, crushing violets in my forest, leaving prints outside my windows, at my threshold.

What is it? I thought. Something had drawn me down the coast into the heart of San Francisco, far away from silence. The apartment I rented was old and disheveled, full of the ghosts of other people's passions. Cut-glass doorknobs, patches in the plaster where things had been thrown. Banging radiators that woke me in the middle of the night to remind me that I was alone in the dark. It was spring. In the small jungle of a garden outside my window camellias bloomed. Roses. Fuchsias. Nasturtiums. Brilliant orange, red, purple colors that glowed even through my closed curtains, even in the dark when I sat on the chipped window ledge, smelling fog, damp roots, brine from the sea winds. Or perfume, on soft nights when the foghorns were still and not even the orange nasturtium petals trembled. *Frances, where are you?* I thought, wanting her, wanting to disappear into her muteness, her tales that were a wall against the world. But I was Frances, and the walls were gone. The night air touched my skin, I breathed fear and longing into my lungs, and I didn't know, anymore, the ending of any tale.

Nothing I did contained any peace. Suddenly even opening a can of tuna fish was an act of urgency, of mystery, leading by some power in the air, or unseen filaments of thoughts, toward other mysteries. Lugging laundry down the street to the laundromat at twilight, I walked through a symphony of impressions. A rag of scarlet where the sun had gone down behind the fog bank building up over the western sea. Chords of hard rock brawling out into the street as a bar door opened suddenly. An Arab face, dark hair, restless dark eyes, dark mustache. A Korean face. Gum, dogshit, cigarette butts on the pavements. Oranges and kiwi fruit on a sidewalk stand. The scent of coffee and tiny white loquat blossoms. Faces. Stagmen. In cutoffs, piling dirty towels into a washing machine. In business suits or blue jeans, smoking in the twilight, waiting for a table in a little Japanese restaurant. Plates, inside, of white rice, raw fish, tiny bowls of sauces. Eyes. Flicking sideways glances at me. Watching, until I looked up, not knowing why, to meet light eyes, dark eyes, smiling slightly, reminding me that I was flesh and bones, existing in this twilight moment. Challenging me to respond.

I had learned a thousand taboos against response. What I had never learned was that the body creates its own language of response, regardless of all the goblins in the mind. I knew my face was changing, but I didn't know that each stagman's glance that touched it pulled hidden things into its surface. I knew that my hands, of their own volition, were becoming sensitive to shapes and textures: smooth oak tables, rose petals, wool, wineglass stems. But I didn't recognize their restless searching. My eyes were drawn to faces, to expressions, beards, laughter lines; something else in me, a sixth sense I had never noticed before, grew tendrils of awareness, scented shades and nuances of feeling from passing strangers that seemed more vivid, somehow, than the quick impression left in the eye. I didn't know what I was looking for, in this world suddenly popu-

lated with stagmen. They all were strangers, and I could
hardly speak, let alone use the language of seduction. But
my body went its own way, fashioning a language for the
mute, leaving me occasionally bewildered by the response.

Pieces of stagmen haunted my dreams. The hollow curve
and hillock of bone in a brown ankle. An earlobe, a pattern
of hair around a nipple, a shaggy eyebrow. Voices, deep,
rough, nuzzling my ear. Legs in tight jeans, in ridiculous
bathing trunks men seemed to wear only in Macy's ads,
in jogging shorts, muscled, hairy, sweating, pale or brown,
short or long, young or old. Stagmen lighting cigarettes,
lifting beer glasses through bar windows, buying soap and
dog food, sitting on streetcars, driving VWs and Ferraris,
dressed in leather and chains, riding motorcycles, bicycles.
Carrying satchels, textbooks, walking their dogs, unloading
boxes off trucks. They were everywhere. On billboards
smoking Marlboros, in the news, running the government,
drilling for oil, making laws, making wars. In the movies,
looking at women, undressing women, slowly or quickly,
undressing each other. They cluttered my head, waking
and sleeping. They shattered my silence. They had always
been there. Why had I never noticed? I had always noticed.
With my brain, with my eyes. Even with longing. But
never before with some stranger waking inside me, full of
irrational and overwhelming impulses, who was slowly turning me into herself.

A third "I." There had been Frances, and there was me.
I. Frances. And now there was a third Frances, whom I
didn't know and couldn't control. And didn't want to
control. Her compulsion was as strong as storytelling, and
far more dangerous. She could barely sit still to write. She

walked streets in the evenings, aware of strangers' glances. She drank alone, late at night, and understood the reasons for the patched dents in the walls. She watched the roses open. She wanted, and there was no philosophy, religion, habit, or fear stopping her. She preferred death to Frances's solitude.

Finally, she found one face that shone back at her with her own shining. I had stopped outside a bar during one of my twilight wanderings. The air was warm, full of vague shimmerings: a city beginning to glow with night. Inside, the bar glittered with chrome and glass, mirrors and chandeliers. Oak tables flushed with soft light, wicker and velveteen couches. A world of elegant possibilities, a haven from cracked walls and smudged paint. It was full of stagmen, drinking, smoking, laughing. They were just a step away beyond the glass. But I was too shy and too proud to acknowledge either their glances or my own loneliness. Then I saw the face behind the bar.

I pushed the door open. Or she pushed the door open, this other Frances, who was compelled to wander into strange territories. What she was going to do inside, I didn't know. The bartender watched her. He wasn't smiling. His face was the face out of a fairy tale: young, dark-eyed, beautiful. It seemed surrounded by light, an aura cast by the reflection of the crystal chandelier in the mirror behind him. His kingdom was a kingdom of bottle and glass; he bestowed wishes in the form of Irish coffee and Jack Daniel's. He polished a wineglass slowly with a white cloth, turning it over and over in his hands, warming it to light. His eyes drew me, out of my shyness, through the smoke and noise and the pound of rock music, up to the bar. His face seemed to mirror my own wonder, as if all the windings and side trails of his unknown past had led him to this place, to this moment.

I sat down in front of him. He put the glass he was drying down very gently and said, "What can I do for you?" The expression in his eyes was changing. The wonder flowing out of him seemed to shift, like light shifting in a prism, into a deeper intensity. I asked for wine; he leaned toward me slightly to hear my voice. Time measured itself to his intensity; brief moments stretched forever, details magnified. His eyes were downcast, lashes longer than mine. Small, taut lines of emotion or hardship deepened slightly at the corner of his mouth. The dark hair was cut crisply along his neck, around his ear. He listened to my order, then raised his head to look at me again. I couldn't meet his eyes any longer. But I felt his attention, as tangible as wind or smoke. His thoughts slowed my thoughts; his gestures spoke to me. His hands, pouring wine, setting a white napkin on the dark glass of the bar, seemed as sensitive to each familiar movement as though they had never touched glass or mahogany before. They told me, in the language of the mute, how he would touch me.

I drank wine, answered his questions, sometimes looking at him, sometimes not. "You're so shy," he said curiously at one point, as though shyness were beyond the realm of his experience, and he wanted to comprehend it, to comprehend me. His desire was like a bass chord, too low to be heard, resonating through me, demanding resolution. My thoughts felt heavy, numbed. I shifted once; his hand came down lightly on my wrist. Stay, it said. He turned to take other orders, talk to other stagmen. I drank more wine, watched the fabric of his shirt mold itself along the muscles of his back as he leaned over the bar. I watched him laugh. The lines rippled away from his smile, giving a curious, tormented depth to the youngness. I couldn't have moved out of his kingdom if I tried. I barely knew him; I barely knew myself anymore. I willed, in my own familiar flesh and bones, a beauty to match his beauty. Maybe I created at least an illusion; when he turned back to me, his expression changed again, as though he, too, saw the stranger in me.

He took me to supper when his shift ended. By that time the unspoken word passed back and forth between us with every breath, every spoken word. I sat, in the Japanese restaurant two blocks from my apartment, with my head bowed over a bowl of udon, trying to scoop foot-long noodles into a spoon, trying to make conversation, trying to think, while my left hand wanted to slide itself over the swell of breast and nipple under his shirt, and my right hand wanted to curve itself behind his head, feel the clean dark hair and warm skin, bring his head down, capture a word leaving his mouth between my lips. The noodles kept slipping off my spoon. I couldn't eat. "Frances," he said softly. "Frances." I couldn't look at him. My own name shot like a lightning pulse in my blood. I wanted him to say my name against me everywhere. To murmur it between my breasts, between my thighs, so that no private corner of me would be nameless.

We walked through the night smelling of loquat blossoms. He reached up silently, broke off a spray, and handed them to me. White flowers, my heart. He lifted my hand, kissed my wrist, held it a moment against him, as though he could feel the blood beat under his lips. He caught my eyes again. My own face dissolved; his face, under the streetlight, seemed only an extension, a reflection of mine. He whispered something; he seemed to move toward me without moving. Or I moved toward him, on a tide without sound. Then we walked again. He took the keys out of my hand, opened my doors for me. As he walked into my apartment, all the cracks and shadows of loneliness fled like mice. I felt at home at last in my own home, the nameless woman who had left the forest in pursuit of a stag, who had returned at last with the prince.

I touched his shirt, the whiteness that my hands had longed toward all evening. I felt the muscles of his shoulders, his back. He looked down at me, his face soft, open. My heart hung like a wind chime in his smile. He pushed the open door half-closed, sliding his other hand into my hair, lifting my face to brush his lips against mine. He opened my mouth with his mouth; his tongue slid among my teeth, tasting of soy sauce and green tea, startling me a little. He searched there for a long moment, then drew back. I opened my eyes. The look of wonder dawned again on his face.

"My God," said the prince. "You're a virgin."

He fled my forest in haste, and I never saw him again.

Damn you, Frances, I raged for days, when I wasn't crying. *Damn you. Damn you. Why didn't you learn what you were supposed to learn when you were thirteen?* I contemplated slashing my wrists; it was apparently easier than losing your virginity, which was as difficult as being hired with no job experience, and how could you get experience without a job? I was imprisoned within the peeling wallpaper and banging radiators. No one would ever rescue me from that loveless place. I lay awake at nights, drinking and listening to the mice scurry within the walls. I would never write again. I would go back to Macy's, or wait on tables, or teach kindergarten. People. I needed people. Laughter, conversation, sex. All the things Frances had so skillfully avoided, hiding herself within her maze of tales. Reviews of her book came, invitations to speak about it. They seemed the ultimate irony. I buried them in drawers, inside other people's novels. I tried to write; I couldn't write. The silence built around me as heavy as fog, obscuring the peaceful glide of sunlight across the old hardwood floors. There was no place on the blank, cracked walls to rest my eyes. They wanted stagmen, and there was a whole city of them outside my door.

The restlessness drove me out again. I wasn't sure what I was looking for, and I didn't know how to find whatever it was. I roamed far, found myself in unexpected places. Staring into windows full of jade and ivory and sidewalk stands of ginger root, bok choy, tofu, water chestnuts. Standing on the marina at sunset, watching freighters, barges, passenger ships coming home from distant ports, other twilights. Walking down Broadway, passing from beautiful Victorian houses with stained-glass windows, to rows of nightclubs looking exhausted in the bright sun, coming alive only in the shadows. The photos of naked dancers in the windows said, "Here be stagmen." But that wasn't what I was looking for either, and I passed on. At the end of one long day I found myself on some street at the top of some hill overlooking North Beach. There was an old stucco church covered with ivy on top of the hill. I sat down wearily on the steps.

Frances, I thought. *This is ridiculous. What are you looking for? What am I looking for?* There was no answer, just a memory of the silence in my house. Wandering among thousands of strangers in the streets had made me feel only more empty. I didn't know what to do, where to go to get away from myself.

People began to go up the steps around me into the church. They dressed in jeans, batiked skirts; I heard their laughter inside. I couldn't remember the last time I'd been to mass. The revolutions of the Second Ecumenical Council had changed the language, the music, and the mysterious distance between a priest and his flock. But the waxy, scented silence had remained, still causing voices to hush instinctively. These people were chattering. So it wasn't a mass. I gathered enough energy to turn my head and look up at the door. There was a purple poster with a smiling, bearded face on it. A purple poet.

An ankle went past me. Brown, lightly hairy, between a frayed jean leg and a tennis shoe. It revived my flagging interest in the world. A pair of boots and a pair of sandals followed the ankle. I roused myself onto my own tired feet and followed them.

I paid a dollar to get down into the church basement. Its chipped walls were covered with posters, and there were enormous pillows all over the floor. A balding poet in a purple knit cap was smiling vaguely, waiting for us to get settled. Some people were so settled among the pillows they seemed to have gone to sleep. I dropped onto one near the

175

door. The ankle beside me was covered with electric blue; the foot, in leather sandals, was ambiguous. Then two stagman's hands set a leather hat on the floor between us.

The poet began to make weird noises abruptly, with a great deal of energy: "La la la ha ds og go n n s sss ssss . . ." It was a poem, he explained, after an interminable amount of glottals, about Watergate. I wondered what kinds of sounds he would make if I sidled out the door. But the stagman beside me murmured in his throat, and I kept still. I liked the murmur. It was bass, light, yet resonant. I wondered what kind of face went with blue socks, sturdy hands, and a leather hat with a peacock's eye in the band. But eyes were dangerous in the forest, so I refrained from looking.

He gave me no choice. At the break for zucchini bread and coffee, before I could get up and leave, he turned to me and said, "That poem about Watergate was profound, wasn't it? It made me want to gag."

I couldn't tell from the expression in his eyes how serious he was. I said tiredly, "It made me want to leave."

He smiled suddenly, and something deep in me jumped. His face was sunburned, clean-lined, almost harsh, like an old Roman bust, and fiercely intelligent. It wasn't the sixth sense of sex his mind flung out like a fishhook, but a suggestion of genius. I wriggled a little on the pillow, but it was no use. Maybe if I didn't talk, he would think me stupid and go away. But his eyes, a light, hard blue, didn't leave my face. He told me his name, Terence, then asked mine. I told him reluctantly. The air between us seemed to go dead for a moment.

"My God." The burn on his face had deepened. "You."

I stared at him. Me, who? Me who lived in an empty house with banging radiators, who prowled city streets looking for a stagman, looking for myself? When he spoke again, there was a shade of diffidence in his voice. "I've read your novel. I've got it in my bookstore."

I said inanely, "Oh." I wanted to explain to him that the book was not my fault, it was something that had happened before I knew any better, and if I had to do it over again, I would be an airline stewardess instead. But he didn't give me a chance. He touched me lightly, already half rising at his own thought.

"Listen. Come with me. Can you come? I'd love to show you my store, talk with you. It's just down the street. We'll have some wine. There's something I've always wanted to understand about the Stagman symbol in your novel. He's such an intense, compelling figure, he seems to mean different things at different times, and I've always wondered what caused you to create him."

The poet was hissing like a radiator as we left. The streets were softly shadowed with twilight. Explaining the Stagman was like trying to swallow a pyramid. I could only chip away at it pebble by pebble, my voice halting, uncertain, half-resentful because of all the things I dared not say. How could I explain a stagman in the middle of a freeway except by temporary insanity? Terence listened closely, watching me speak as we walked, encouraging me with small noises. Finally he said, touching me again, "It's all right. God, I'm asking you to explain intuition by logical processes. It even makes sense that you're so shy. Of course you would be; that's why you write." He unlocked the door to his store, flung it open, and walked in, leaving me standing at the threshold, feeling as though I'd just seen him deflate a tornado with a pin. He flicked on the lights, reached behind the counter for a bottle of wine and glasses. He glanced at me surprisedly. "Come in. Come in."

He had collected everything in his store. Shelves, rising to the ceiling of classics, poetry journals, French and South American novels, modern drama, science, psychology, science fiction, romances. There was a whole stand in the middle of the floor dedicated to politics and economy.

"Sit, sit, sit."

I sat down slowly on a box of unpacked books. "What am I sitting on?"

"*A Hundred Years of Solitude.*" He gave me wine. "Twenty-five copies. I couldn't afford more. Absolutely incredible novel. Do you like it? My book store? I started it three years ago, when I graduated." He reached behind him, switched on a stereo. Baroque music filled the store, gave the gold wine an antique glow. He listened a moment, head cocked, then looked at me again, smiling, sharing his pride in himself, his pleasure in my company. His feelings reached out to me like hands, drawing me into them, warming me like the wine, until I realized I was giving his own smile back to him.

We drank wine and talked about books, or I listened to him talk, while it grew dark outside and the city became ethereal with light. Part of my mind detached itself, roamed over him curiously, watched his pale, short lashes, his hands gesturing, the triangle of sunburn at his neck. His body looked strong, muscular, like a piece of statuary. Was it burned all over, I wondered, or pale as marble? Terence, I thought. Terence. It suited him. Masculine, vaguely classical. He put his glass down, letting a sudden silence fall, and I wondered if he'd read my mind. The silence lengthened; he stared down at his glass, drew a breath as if to ask me something, tell me something. But he didn't. The locked door opened so suddenly we both started.

A young man came in, with a key in his hand. He was tall, with blond, windblown hair and eyes clear and serene as water. They went to me and then to Terence. He smiled lightly, and I realized he was a little drunk. We all were a little drunk.

"Justin." Terence shifted to get up, but Justin held him down, a hand on his shoulder.

"I'll get it." He reached behind the counter for another wineglass. As he poured, I watched a bracelet on his wrist flare red-gold in the light. There seemed to be an intricate pattern on it, strange writing, maybe, telling a circular tale. I said involuntarily, "That's beautiful. Is it gold?"

He nodded, the light smile still on his lips. "It was a gift from a woman in Morocco. I'd been wandering around there. I walked into her village, and she gave me tea on a copper tray and the bracelet, for no reason."

Terence made a noise in his throat. His face had changed very slightly; I could feel the intensity of his attention, but I couldn't guess what, without words, he was trying to tell me. He introduced us, and Justin leaned down, brushed a kiss on my cheek. He swallowed wine and surveyed us again. "How long have you been talking? Hours? Have you eaten? No? Come, children. The night is young, and the carriage is illegally parked outside the door. Let's savor the pleasures of the city."

Terence's body shifted, the energy of his ideas draining

out of it, leaving it loose, still powerful, yet oddly vulnerable to pleasure or trouble. He eyed me a moment, saw me smiling foolishly at the prospect of good company and adventure in the city's night. So he shrugged and said, "Why not?" He took my hand gently, surprising me, and drew me to my feet. "Be careful with this one," he said to Justin. "She doesn't have any gold bracelets, and she'll put us in a novel if we don't behave."

Justin laughed and started asking questions. In the spring night, with the moon cradling itself just above the Transamerica Building, I somehow found my voice. They made me feel happy, attractive. We fitted ourselves into a black Porsche. Justin drove. His bracelet burned in every streetlight. I sat on Terence's lap, my face dangerously close to the windshield, turned to watch Justin's fine profile, smiling faintly as the power flared from his wrist. He and Terence talked about Europe, about someone named Alex who had gone to Amsterdam for a week and stayed three years, about Africa. And as Terence said that word, I heard, clear as the bellow of foghorns over the bay, the longing in his voice for adventure.

We stopped for vegetarian food and then for drinks along the way, in a bar with oak tables and Boston ferns, whose waitresses knew Justin. I drank too much vodka, and as the Porsche bounced and swooped up and down hills at one-fifteen, I could only put my hands against the windshield and plead ineffectually, laughing. They left the car next to a fire hydrant and followed the sounds of jazz into a bar. The musicians' faces seemed genderless as angels in a Botticelli painting. A black hatcheck girl in chartreuse hot pants winked at Justin as we walked by. She seemed six feet tall, sinewy, indrawn, melting into lines and smoky shadows to the music.

Justin bought us more drinks; I took one sip of mine, and then his fingers linked around my wrist, while he took the glass from my hand. "Dance with me."

A sphere of jagged mirrors revolved over our heads as we danced. Faces seemed blurred around me, nothing quite clear. With their cropped hair and heavy make-up they seemed masklike. Once I stared without knowing why at a couple kissing. Justin asked me, "Does it bother you?"

"No," I said, surprised. "Why should it?" The next dance was slow; I went back to the bar to get Terence. He set his glass down almost reluctantly. There was an odd expression on his face, but he said nothing for a while, only held me gently as we danced. I realized then, with an odd amazement, how much I needed to be held by another human being. Several times I felt him gather breath. Finally, he broke his silence.

"Justin told me he thought you are very poised and beautiful."

I made a surprised noise against his shoulder. "He did? That was nice."

"Yes." He paused. Something stuck in his throat; he cleared it, then ran a hand down my hair. "I suppose you guessed that once he was my lover."

Something was happening. I pulled back from Terence in astonishment, to see his eyes, then felt something nudge against me. Terence pulled at me; I moved mechanically, then looked down. Justin was rolling on the floor under a woman bigger than he was. As I stared at her, the woman's face changed. Beneath the heavy powder, the bones were too big; the shinbones were too long; the pale, painted hands gripping Justin's shirt were too big. A waiter with a tray of drinks put it down hastily and said between his teeth, "God damn it—get them out of here!" The hatcheck girl, who was afflicted with the same incongruity of bone, and a sturdy bouncer pulled the men apart. Terence helped Justin up, held him while the light flickered wildly over still, masked faces, and an electric guitar, catching a seven chord tossed to it by the string bass, played it into an imperative crescendo, like a desperate question.

I closed my eyes. When I opened them again, all the women in the room had turned into men. Magic. The back of my throat made another noise. Then Terence took my arm, pulling at Justin with his other hand.

"Let's get out of here." In the street Justin tugged at his rumpled shirt and smiled crookedly.

"I'm sorry," he said. "I just felt like fighting. You know me." He unlocked the Porsche unsteadily. "Better get out of here before she comes back. Where can I drop you?"

"Here," Terence said. "We'll walk."

Justin looked at him, the smile dying away finally into faint uncertainty. Then he turned, gave me one brief, dry kiss. The Porsche squealed away from the curb; I gazed after it for some reason until the taillights disappeared over a hill. I drew a breath. Terence was silent beside me. I wished he were anywhere else, under the curb, on the dark side of the moon. I whispered, "Jesus Christ."

"I'm sorry," Terence said. "I shouldn't have let you come. Justin attracts trouble like a magnet. Frances. Frances." He put his hand on my shoulder. "Frances." I looked at him finally. His face seemed far away, in another world.

He said very softly, "I'm sorry." I couldn't answer. "Talk to me. Talk about it."

I couldn't talk. I had fled one dangerous world, only to find myself in another one, extremely complicated, uncertain, and far more dangerous, where it seemed nothing, not even the faces of stagmen, could be taken for granted. I couldn't go back, and suddenly I was terrified of going forward. I said finally, in a small, high voice I didn't recognize, "I think I'm lost."

Stagmen. Men. There was a bewildering, astonishing variety of them, with minds as various as their faces. Sitting a few days later in my window, watching cats prowl in the night garden, watching occasional bearded faces pass the lit windows around me, I thought about illusions and reality, and the endings of fairy tales. *Once upon a time* . . . *And they lived happily ever after.* . . . True love. Romance. Passion. Beautiful women dressed in black velvet gowns on billboards promised all those things and more. Women had pursued stagmen, and stagmen had pursued women since the beginning of time. But what had they been pursuing? I was looking for a stagman, but the vision in my head didn't seem to have much to do with the men I was encountering. The Stagman was part of me, not part of the world around me. There was nothing in a dream or a lady on a billboard that could put its arms around you and hold you because you were a human being, alive, and in need of holding. Yet the vision was in my head, as strong and ambiguous as ever, and the lady was on the billboard, rising over the freeway, making silent promises to the thousands of drivers stuck in morning traffic jams. They were gods, the Stagman and the Black Velvet Lady. I thought of the vital, aggressive energy I had loved in the bartender, of Terence's intelligence. These things drew me, beyond reason. I wanted to become part of them. Maybe I had invented the Stagman to contain a wildness, a passion, a fearlessness that had no other outlet in my own fearful life.

I held that thought, like a mouthful of strange wine, in my head. If it was true, maybe there was some hope for Frances. Maybe the Stagman had been, sometimes, the only part of myself I could like. I mused over that, feeling in the soft evening, on the verge of peace. Or an illusion of peace. Then the doorbell buzzed.

It was the outer door, someone on the street wanting me. I had no idea who it might be. I opened my door, looked downstairs, but I couldn't see much beyond the panes of glass in the outer door. I went downstairs, opened the door. There was no one on the porch. I stepped out, looked up and down the sidewalk. An old woman, two girls, a kid on a skateboard. I turned to go back in. And stopped, staring at a locked door.

I had, I realized suddenly, not only locked myself out of the building but closed my apartment door behind me, and it had locked itself. Anyone in the building could let me in the front door, but only the managers had a spare key to my apartment. I pushed their button, panicked at being stranded on the street at nine at night. No response. I pushed it again. But they were out, too, somewhere in the warm spring night. I felt tears sting my eyes. A stranger wandering by had interrupted my peace, pulled me out of my house, and gone, while the house shut itself up behind me like some medieval fortress pulling up its bridge at sundown. Then I smelled the perfume from the loquat flowers and heard lovers' laughter from a couple across the street. The strange peace began to drift back into me. There seemed a touch of calculation to the moment. But whose calculation, and what the moment might bring, I couldn't guess. I turned, followed the air, to find a place to wait for my key.

I passed the bar where I had met the bartender, without looking in the window to see if he was there. I passed a couple of coffee shops, both closed, and some small restaurants that were on the verge of closing. There was a pizza parlor, an ice-cream shop. And there was music.

I stopped. Somebody was playing a classical guitar in a corner bar. The windows opened up along the sidewalk; I could see polished tables and wicker couches, people talking quietly or listening to the guitar player. It seemed a friendly place to spend a tranquil evening; perhaps they would let a penniless, homeless neighbor rest there for a while. I went in, found an empty couch in the shadows. After a moment I stole a cautious glance at the bartender. She was a pretty, red-haired lady, who seemed to be adopting a motherly attitude toward all her customers. I settled back to watch the guitar player.

He was tall, with broad shoulders under a white home-spun shirt and a lean, hard, hawklike face, absolutely intent on his work. I could feel the force of his concentration across the room. His music was precise and flawless, with an edge of raw, fiery energy. I closed my eyes after a moment and thought, *No. No. No.* He was the closest I had ever been to the Stagman. But I was learning slowly that the Stagman was part of my own shadow, or my dreams, to be endlessly pursued, endlessly challenging, forcing the best of strength, creativity, passion from me. If caught, it became something else, and I was left unsatisfied, still in pursuit. For the moment I was content to linger in my peace and let the Stagman be. A voice said, "What can I get you to drink?"

I opened my mouth, then remembered I had no money, no identification, not even a Kleenex. I began explaining; the waitress was laughing before I finished. "No problem," she said. "I do that to myself all the time. You can wait here as long as you need to."

I thanked her, warmed by her understanding. Before she could turn, another voice from behind a lamp on the table next to me asked diffidently, "Can I buy you a drink?"

I peered beyond the light. A small, bearded man smiled at me. His face reminded me of both a leprechaun and Santa Claus. The nose, nicely tilted, was the leprechaun, I decided; the cheekbones above his beard were Santa Claus. There were laughter lines at the corners of his eyes; his smile was harmless, unromantic, and kind.

The waitress looked questioningly at me. I asked for wine; she smiled a benison and withdrew. The man moved himself and his beer to the couch beside me. He wasn't much taller than I was, but stronger, stockier. He was dressed in jeans and a plaid shirt that applied itself nicely to his shoulders. On a street I would never have noticed him. Sitting beside him, I felt his warmth. He was quiet until the guitar player ended his song, and then he asked, "Have you heard him play before? I came to the city tonight especially to listen to him. I'd love to learn guitar. All I play is this."

He produced a harmonica from his pocket. It brought back childhood memories, making me smile. I took it, turned it over in my hands, thinking back. "I can play 'Oh! Susanna!' and 'Jingle Bells.' "

He laughed, his own shyness disappearing. "Those are the two songs everyone learned when they were ten."

"And 'Amazing Grace.' "

" 'Amazing Grace'? Where'd you pick that up?"

"I don't remember." I gave it back to him. "Where do you live?"

"On the coast, in Half Moon Bay. On a bus."

I swallowed wine quickly. "On a bus?"

"On a hundred acres of land. Belongs to my mother. She and my grandmother live in the house; I live on the bus on the edge of the hayfield."

I studied him, wondering if men would ever cease amazing me. "A bus. Is it comfortable?"

"Sure. I've got it all fixed up. Stove, water, bed, refrigerator. An electric blanket, even a pint-sized TV. I love it. I wake up in the mornings, prop the emergency door open with a broom, and all the morning smells—the hay and the trees and the sea mist—come right in with me. It's like camping." He paused; in the moment I imagined waking up on his bus, smelling his morning. He added, "I could never live in the city. I'm a farmer, from a long line of farmers. Parents, grandparents, great-grandparents . . ." He swigged beer. "Your basic lower-class farmer."

He gave me something new to mull over. "Classes."

"Life is full of pecking orders. What do you do?"

I told him. He nodded, a little shy again. "I figured you for an artist of some kind. They're different. A class of their own." He gestured with the beer at the guitar player. "Like that one. You know the music?"

I nodded. *Asturias,* by Albénez. It was running through me almost painfully, with all its urgent mysteries. The mystery lay in the guitar player, not in the man beside me. But at that moment the small man beside me had something I needed more. He was watching me as I sipped wine and listened.

"You have a real pretty smile," he said. "It's nice and warm. But I get the feeling you haven't been using it much. You're locked out of your apartment until the managers get back, and there's no one inside your house to let you in."

I looked at him. Then I set my wineglass down carefully and said, "I think I'm going to cry."

"That's okay. That's what bars are for." He leaned over suddenly, put his arm around my shoulders briefly, and kissed my cheek. "That's a hug. People need to be hugged."

I wiped at tears with my cuff, half laughing. "Do you have a name? Or do you just go around hugging people?"

"Will," he said. His voice, giving his name, was a comforting combination of shyness and strength. "Go ahead. Have some more wine and talk. You're having a rough time in the city. Tell me about it."

I told him. Two or three glasses of wine later, after the conversation had turned to his own broken marriage, then strayed into organic farming, he stopped in midsentence and said simply, looking away from me, "That bartender friend of yours was a fool."

I was silent. The guitar player was playing softly, dreamily; the bar was nearly empty. I had no idea what time it was, but the apartment managers were probably home. I could get my key, go to bed. Will seemed to sense my thought, as easily as he sensed other things. He touched my shoulder. "You want me to walk you home?"

"I'll be all right. It's just down the street."

"What if you can't get back in?"

"I'll be okay."

"Okay." He seemed to draw away from me a little; he sat silently a moment, looking down at his callused hands. Then he hugged me again. "Good night, darlin'. You're a beautiful woman, and that bartender needs his head examined. Remember that."

I watched him cross the bar, looking small and unremarkable in the light from the guitar player's dais. The guitar player's dark, hard, intense gaze focused on him as he moved. Then it switched to me, looking through me and beyond me, frowning slightly, in curiosity or reproach, as if a tale he had heard all evening beneath his playing had stopped without ending.

My body stood up. Will was taking all the warmth out of the room with him. I didn't want to be left without it. I caught up with him at the door, turned him with a hand on his shoulder. His face seemed politely surprised; he didn't meet my eyes. I said, suddenly uncertain, "I just wanted to thank you. For listening to me. I needed some kindness."

He met my eyes then. His shyness left him, and I felt his warmth again, simple, uncomplicated, worthy of trust. He linked his fingers into mine, pushed the door open. "You don't need your key," he said softly. "Not tonight. Come play me a song while we drive to the sea."

8 ~ TWO SISTERS

A year later I drove to a different sea. I. Frances. Driving by myself across an entire continent, when once I could hardly bring myself to walk alone into a shoe store. My mind took amazed Polaroid images of myself along the way. Frances. An unobtrusive figure wandering across a map in a small blue car, not even knowing what a carburetor was. Stopping to rest among the brilliant, crackling pines of the Sierras, beneath a billboard of Uncle Sam blowing out two hundred birthday firecrackers on a cake. Pounding tent pegs with a hatchet in a hard, dusty KOA camp in Reno. Feeding nickels into an insatiable one-armed bandit. Sitting in a moonlit cherry orchard in Salt Lake City, on an evening so still she could practically hear the cherries ripening, watching a movie run by the Morman campground owners about Joseph Smith and the Angel Moroni. Sitting on a weird rock-cropping in Wyoming, playing one of two songs she knew on a flute made out of glass and wondering why the civilization she belonged to had wrought nothing more profound than Stuckey's in the charged, eerie wilderness of space. Eating a hot dog at Stuckey's. Watching a local talent show in a tiny Nebraska town, with everyone dressed as a cowboy or saloon girl. Driving past an old oak tree in Iowa with a yellow ribbon tied around it. Sleeping in a rest area in Michigan, curled in the front seat, surrounded by the comfortable, purring motors of semis. Getting lost on side roads in Canada at sundown, looking for gas. Staring down the glassy green waters of Niagara Falls that poured so silently, so smoothly toward nothingness, luring her eyes with its still, constant movement toward its own disappearance, toward the moment when it slipped soundlessly down over an edge of serenity and roared its terrifying, powerful existence. Frances, tired, defenseless, made invulnerable by her own obliviousness to danger. Leaving only a moment's impression on the eye: a young woman, a stranger, belonging somewhere else. Not here in Laramie, or here in Omaha, or here in Detroit, but belonging somewhere else, just getting ready to leave here and go there, wherever it was that had produced her. Driving at last, under a rainbow placed no doubt by the Massachusetts Chamber of Commerce, into a tiny, elegant portion of land where time warped and flowed back into itself, and yesterdays still existed in the rooms and cornices of old houses,

in cemeteries, in patches of strangely troubled or untrou-
bled air. Navigating instinctively, knowing that lands' ends
are worshiped, compelled to the farthest point of Cape Cod
before I finally stopped.

At rest, at morning, I lay in my tent listening to foghorns
and frogs. New England frogs droned like bellows in deep
bass voices. The foghorns at the end of Cape Cod played a
lovely major triad. The notes sounded sporadically, sometimes only one, sometimes all three, lingering, overlapping
to the rhythm of fog and tide, while the frogs produced a
shadowy continuo. I stirred finally, poked my head out the
tent flap, to be met with a vision of blank, drifting sky,
gray-white sand, and a moment of the past, woken, probably, by all the celebrations of history. A small ship full of
Pilgrims peered bewilderedly back at me through the mist.
But they found no stone in the barren sandy shore to take
their one small step for mankind, so they continued to
Plymouth.

I got dressed, also on my way to Plymouth. As I took
down my tent, the morning sun rose over the wrong ocean,
making me homesick. The Atlantic had a sluggish, dour
voice, like an old barnacled philosopher; I missed the
rugged, sinewy voice of the West Coast. Pausing, my tent
sagging, I took a swig of scotch for breakfast and toasted
the unknown world.

I drove around the Cape Cod curl, away from the sun,
and reached Plymouth a couple of hours later. I was on
time to watch the ship come in. As I gazed down with other
tourists at the small rock surrounded by chicken wire, a
boot cracked and blackened with bilge water came down on

it, swung away. A child was sick. Somebody swatted a mosquito. A mist rolled inland, obscuring the merciless view of scrub and sand. A voice whispered like a prayer: "What in God's name are we doing here?"

In Boston, munching cannoli, I listened to arguments about life, liberty, and the pursuit of men's happiness. In Concord I stood in a small green park surrounded by old, quiet trees. The bronze statue of a minuteman in the middle of it lifted his gun and fired a shot heard 'round the world, causing me to choke on a bite of my clamburger. Everywhere in New England were remnants of a two-hundred-year-old celebration of war. The napkin my clamburger came wrapped in was imprinted with the lean, bearded visage of Uncle Sam. I couldn't remember, suddenly, when I had learned his name, why he had come into being. He had always been there, somebody's uncle, somebody's myth, like Halloween or Thanksgiving turkeys. A symbol, like the blurring memory of the Stagman in my head, inspiring the irrational, the impossible, then losing its power and fading into the general familiarity of life, along with all the other worn-out gods, to become a face on a nickel or a clamburger napkin. In Salem I stood in the middle of a sidewalk, shaken by a hollow wind.

The air was the color of gravestones, sullen and booming like the sea. Angels above tombs, no more than round faces with great, round eyes, seemed to stare through the wind, seeing shadows. I went into one of the gray gabled houses left over from a distant age. A girl with skin fine-grained as marble, with gray eyes that stared through me, said, "The tour through the house of the witch trials will begin in ten minutes. . . ." She was dressed in Pilgrim black and white. Her eyes seemed to smile at something which wasn't funny at all.

I sat down. Another Pilgrim guide sat down beside me; her hands, slender and tallow-pale, played at cat's cradle. I watched the constant shift of angles between her fingers. My mind filled with angles; I blinked to keep myself awake. Then I noticed the flame at the center of the angles, small and calm, a candle flame. The string flared suddenly; all the changing angles were of fire, clinging to the girl's hands. I jumped. A tired voice said, "I did no magic. There is no magic. Is there?" The rest of the tour was uneventful.

I arrived at my final destination two days later: an old farm in Massachusetts turned into an artists' colony. Angels gazed at me from the tiny cemetery across the road. Country roads led into the twilight around me, between small farms and houses, through thick forests of yellow birch. Hounds bayed in the distance. Someone in a field played a flute.

I had come, as an artist among other artists, to write. What I might be writing I didn't know. I seemed to be hovering between two tales: the ending of one and the beginning of another. I leaned against the car tiredly, feeling as warm and dusty as it was. The white shuttered farmhouse, surrounded by huge trees, looked as though it had passed into a tranquil old age, full of friendly ghosts and no dark shadows. An artist was sitting on the front lawn, painting the lingering sunset over the birch wood.

I went over to her, not knowing where else to go. She glanced at me, then ducked her head down quickly, frowning at her paints. She was small-boned and thin, like a child; her face seemed plain, until I spoke to her, and she looked up again, bird-shy, half-frightened, yet trying to smile. Her eyes were enormous, gray as dove feathers, promising visions.

I told her my name and asked what I should do with my suitcase. She moved a little jerkily, knocking a paintbrush down, searching for her voice.

"I don't know. Where you're staying. Someone knows. Tom, I think his name is Tom." She paused, all her nervousness fading a moment as she gazed critically at her magenta birch trees. Then her attention came back to me as I stood there blankly. "Oh. Tom is— There'll be supper in a few minutes. They ring a bell. You can find out then."

"Where is supper? Here?"

"No, it's behind the graveyard."

"We eat with the witches?"

She gave me a little sudden smile. She was my age, I realized. Maybe older, though with the lines of worry and scrutiny under her eyes, it was hard to tell. "No. Down the road." She gestured, nearly getting her brush tangled in her muddy hair. "You have a car. You can park—" Her voice, grating, hesitant, smoothed suddenly with wonder. "You drove all the way from California? All by yourself? I could never do that. Never. How did you do it?"

"I'm not so sure myself," I confessed. I stood a little longer, watching her paint. Then shutters from upstairs in the farmhouse banged open, and a young, wild-haired, bare-breasted woman leaned out, laughing.

"Shana! Shana!" The artist turned, her small, sallow face lighting nearly to beauty with her smile. "Come see what that bloody monkey of yours did to my paint box!"

The artist disappeared into the farmhouse. I heard their

laughter within the walls. Friends, I thought. Or lovers. Or sisters. One with a monkey instead of a bird. A little shiver ran through me, not of cold or of fear. Of premonition, maybe, or recognition. Or both.

A bell rang, like an angelus. People came out of the farmhouse. The two friends, their arms over each other's shoulders. A slender gray-haired man. A pretty dark-haired woman with a ten-year-old beside her. A big, friendly-looking woman with an Aztec face, a graying braid down her back, paint splashes all over her smock. A small red-haired man with a parrot on his shoulder and a jangle of keys at his belt. I followed them past a stand of evergreens, and an apple orchard, to a big stone building at the bottom of the road. The smell of bread and stew mingled with the twilight smells. More people were already inside, seated at long monkish tables. The noise and laughter, the combined energy of thirty-odd writers, musicians, painters rolled toward me like an exuberant wave and stopped me at the threshold. I could feel myself turning pale, shadowy, invisible. Right now they were a force, but soon enough, I reminded myself patiently, they could become individuals, each face imprinted with its own peculiar courage and frustration. I stepped into the room, sat down at the first empty chair I could find, between the only woman in the room wearing lipstick and the small man with the parrot.

Fresh bread, big bowls of boiled kale, salad, and beef stew circled the tables. The woman, passing me bread, glanced at me and smiled. The parrot cast a cold, dubious eye upon me and squawked.

"Silence, Birdbrain," the small man commanded.

"Oh, you shouldn't call him that," a beautiful blonde

with the sloe-eyed secret face of a Botticelli virgin, chided him, and I realized the two sisters were at the table with me. The parrot's owner attacked kale imperturbably.

"That's his name. Granted," he added, swallowing, "he might call himself something completely different in the privacies of his own language, but since he belongs to me, feather body and bird wit, he's at my mercy for his name."

"Just like a child," the woman beside me said suddenly. "My parents named me Hilary. I think it was the sexual confusion of being called Larry by my peers for the first twelve years of my life that drove me into the convent. Naming is such a dangerous power."

The small man smiled. "My parents named me Michael. Michael Thaddeus O'Brian. It didn't keep me from being sexually confused anyway."

"A good Irish Catholic name," a gray-haired man with an elegant face commented.

"Isn't it so? I was absolutely in love with the crucified Christ until I was fourteen. Then I switched my devotion to my algebra teacher, a man with a Christ-like face, who was utterly shocked when I confessed my passion. I contemplated suicide, but found the devil and painting were more interesting." He reached for the kale bowl. I swallowed a lump of bread and butter. It was the strangest dinner conversation I had ever encountered. It was making me apologetic for my own poor sorrows, like a child opening a box of private treasures in front of adults and seeing it suddenly through their eyes: a frayed dead butterfly, a few dusty sea stones, a tarnished key to nothing, a bell off a bicycle that still gave a rusty ring.

198

"I did my doctoral thesis when I was in the Jesuit semi-nary," the elegant man said, "on the subconscious fascina-tion the creative mind has—or had in earlier centuries—for the devil. Now, of course, the power of the symbol has died out among intelligent people—"

"But not the guilt," the woman beside me said abruptly.

"Oh, no. Everyone has his—her—own private and irra-tional hell closet of guilt. But we go to therapists now to be absolved of guilt, as once we went to priests to be absolved of sin. The great modern sin is guilt itself. It's an amazing shift of a civilization's social conscience. So we relegate our gods and devils to gather dust in the attic."

"And the passion and fear along with them," Michael said, "that infect you along with braces and acne."

Hilary looked at him. Her hair was short and dark; her eyes were a lovely, very calm blue. "It can last far longer than acne." She laughed suddenly, a free, happy laugh. "After fifteen years among the Sisters of Notre Dame de Namur I walked out the convent doors feeling like the oldest living virgin. I had to cope with job interviews, rent applications, income taxes, loneliness, guilt, terror of being without faith, without commandments, parallel parking, and tipping for the first time in my life and, on top of that, the fact that the average thirteen-year-old probably knew more about sex than I did. Luckily there are a few gentle men left in the world."

"What do you do?" the beautiful sister asked curiously.

"I teach piano. I came here to try composing for the first time." She laughed again. "Once more a virgin, and just as scared. But I want to try it."

"It was you in the field playing the flute," the dark sister said suddenly, in her tight, gruff voice. She looked startled at the sound and promptly frowned at her stew.

"Guilty. Not very well either. But I wanted to try that, too."

"You wore that violet blouse. Against the green grass. With all the buttercups around you."

"Buttercups," Michael said exuberantly. The parrot nibbled on his ear. "God, I love them. Chalices, love cups, moist, golden kisses. I could eat them, smear them on my body, burn oak wood with them— What is your name?" he said abruptly, turning to me. I had almost forgotten I existed, so I had to grope a moment.

"Frances Stuart."

"Frances Stuart. You have gold rings around your irises the color of buttercups."

There seemed only one rejoinder to that. "Just like your parrot."

"Eyes that see." He nodded toward the dark sister. "You and she—amazing eyes. Where have they been, those eyes? In what grave countries? I'd like to paint everything you've seen."

I thought of the Stagman suddenly for the first time in months. How bizarre it was to have invented, loved, hated, killed, and resurrected a private god, while the world went about its daily business, toppling governments and building McDonald's hamburger stands. The dark sister caught my eye with her curious artist's eye. Then she blushed slightly, and we shared a smile, acknowledging kinship.

I pushed my chair back, tired, wanting to be away from faces, voices, half-buried memories. I wanted to unpack; I wanted scotch; I wanted to stand at the very edge between twilight and night and hear the fading of one into the other.

"I need somebody named Tom," I said, suddenly liking the sound of my own voice.

Michael pointed with a bread crust, counterpointing my lightness with his rich tenor. "Ah. Our camp director. Yon gorgeous fair-haired hulk, speaking to the Jewish princess with the bracelets."

I wandered vaguely the direction his bread crust pointed, not having his eye for distinctions. I found a blond man talking to the dark-haired woman with the child. She wore no wedding ring, and I could only begin to guess at the myriad difficulties in her past. Tom told me where to park, where to find a bed. I reparked the car, lugged my suitcase into the farmhouse, upstairs into a small room overlooking the graveyard. I unpacked paper and pens, laid them on the battered desk, and stood a moment, wondering what new tale the coming summer would bring into my head. Then I unpacked the scotch and a coffee cup from my camping gear. I poured myself a cup, then descended again into the evening.

Rough homespun angels, all grim Protestant eyes and wings, watched me as I entered the tiny graveyard. Grass and wild roses obscured the stones. I touched one angel hovering protectively over the narrow tomb of a five-year-old. Patience Cummings. 1794–1799. At One with God and at Rest. I had a vision of all the stone angels in all the death fields in the land winging through the air as night touched them, to return again at daylight to be frozen into stone by forgetfulness. Yesterday's gods. I drank scotch and turned down the paved, meandering road. Beyond the woods marking the farm boundaries, fences and fields flowed toward the dark, shadowed Berkshires, their lines breaking, seeping into the night. In the dark, stagmen, lovers, ghosts, and homeless poets roamed, searching for beginnings and endings, for understandings, for rest.

The moon rose, setting the distant hills afire with silver. I stopped, entranced, until its luminous aura wore away, and it was just the moon again, and I wondered how many generations of humans, growing away from their primitive adolescence, it would take before even poets saw it with technology's passionless eye. I toasted the moon with my coffee cup and followed it down the road. Fireflies orbited around me in delicate, flickering constellations. The fields swam with light and shadow. Crickets marked my presence; the road, dimpled and blurred like water, suffered my passage. I sprinkled a libation of scotch on it and on the stiff, unblown moons of dandelion seed, the ivory barley stocks. A cow mooed; a small dog yapped once. There is a tower, I remembered, in Ireland or Wales or Avalon, that you may or may not go into, and if you survive to come back out, you will be either mad or a poet. Either or. Cucku or creator. Bananas or inspired. I gave the closed daisy heads a wet libation. Then I came to the house where the hounds lived.

Their rough, hoarse voices warned me against coming closer. But they were chained to the barn, and something dark that wasn't a hound stood silently beyond the fence. It drew me; I leaned against the wood. The vague light drew it slowly. Horns, cloven hooves . . . a black goat, watching me silently out of slitted yellow eyes. I felt the

202

chilly, ancient recognition of its divinity. Goat-god. I backed away from it, raised my cup.

"Cheers."

The hounds' voices pursued me down the road, but I had paid my homage and escaped. The road led out of the fields, skirted the woods. My feet took me into the trees. The birch leaves hung still; the yellow bark peeled on the trunk, parchment for poets. I burrowed against a tree, wanting something to hug, put my cheek against satiny, scratchy bark. I closed my eyes. The night behind my eyelids swam drunkenly with trees, and I opened them again hastily. I drank and moved deeper into the woods.

Pockets of shadow lay where the trees gathered thickly, blocking the moonlight. I tangled in ivy, brambles, tripped over fallen logs, always balancing the cup. Fragments of stories I had told through the years came back to me. Once upon a time there were two sisters . . . there were Hell-Giants, their trapped green saguaro fingers reaching for the stars . . . there were boars, stags, there was a stag-man, there was a god . . . What had my mind been saying to me? What tale was I really telling?

"Once upon a time," I whispered, and felt in my veins, like a streak of lightning, the ancient seduction of imagination. So what happens next, storyteller? Does the king's daughter wander drunk into the forest, and how does she find her way out? Something rustled in the bushes near me: a boar with tusks of blood and moonlight, a stagman with an owl in his horns, something else. What?

The trees were beginning to thin; I caught glimpses of a moonlit field between them, and a light-glazed fence. I stumbled through roots and shrubs, cleared the forest fi-

nally, and hung on the fence a moment before I climbed it
and sat down. The moon reeled a little above me, no longer
mysterious, no longer virgin, tiny instruments and fly-
specks of footprints on its flowing, battered face. The footprints had given dimension to the night; the horizon of
history no longer stopped at the earth's edge. My mind
reached out, imagining distances, darknesses, impossibili-
ties, until I felt myself lurch on the wall. I slid down and
heard, seemingly all around me, disembodied cries of
passion.

I stood blinking, half-sobered, feeling caught in an eerie
dream. The sound continued without climaxing, from the
trees, or from the green field, I couldn't tell. I moved forward
uncertainly, silently across the grass. The sound stopped
abruptly. Two shadows separated almost at my feet.

"Frances Stuart."

I stood still, smelling the scotch I had spilled on myself,
hearing my heart pound. *I'm defined,* I thought surprisedly.
A woman rose from the ground, wearing a long skirt and
no blouse. Her hair looked like a pale, curly dandelion in
the moonlight; the skin of her breasts was very white. It
was the beautiful sister, smiling, secret-eyed, imperturb-
able.

"That's who you are."

"Me?" I said, bewildered and embarrassed. "Who am I?"

"You wrote that book. You. I thought I recognized you."

"Oh. I'm sorry. I didn't mean to—I'm just a little drunk,
and I was following the moon. I'm sorry—" Her eyes smiled
slowly; her hands rose, rested lightly on my shoulders, and
I stopped babbling. Behind her, the mute sister sat like a

204

shadow in the shadows, watching. Dressed, holding a cup between my breasts, I felt vulnerable before their moonlit nakedness.

"You are in your night walk."

"Yes." I met her eyes finally, felt the tension ease out of my shoulders. She brushed her slender hand lightly across my cheek, and I saw, with a second shock, some recognition of beauty, or a moonlit illusion of it, in her eyes. But the gift she gave me with the touch of her fingers was free; she asked no price for it. I stayed still; her hands moved finally, lifted as lightly as they had fallen.

"We're staying in the cabin at the edge of the woods," she said. "Come visit us if you like."

She kissed my cheek, drifted back into the shadows. The field was very quiet as I crossed it. The night was quiet, even the hounds. *Just people,* I thought. Then I thought, *I think.* Who knows when an oak tree or a woman will suddenly lose all its familiarity to shine with some force from your mind, as a warning or a beacon or a message? A piece of your tale. A beginning. Or an ending.

I came to a stone wall, drank the last of the scotch. I had walked miles, but I had made a circle. The wall bordered the orchards beside the farmhouse, and the lights just ahead of me were the lights of home.

I bumped into a leg and heard a laugh, then a squawk. My heart jumped again; then I laughed. Michael Thaddeus O'Brian, with Birdbrain on his shoulder, was sitting on the wall, contemplating the moon. I heaved myself up beside him. His hands were full of buttercup petals. He showered them over me suddenly.

"Shake your head," he commanded.

I shook it, and all the petals showered out, caught on my clothes, in the stones. He sighed contentedly.

"Thanks. I needed that." I shifted, brushing against his shoulder, wanting to be close to his voice, his maleness, even though the pleasure of his voice would be the only thing he could give me. But he surprised me, putting his arm over my shoulders, giving me a tight, friendly hug.

"Thanks," I said after a moment. "I needed that. I tried a tree, but it wasn't the same."

"A tree's no good substitute on a night of a full moon. Neither is a parrot," he added wryly. "But for the moment that's all I've got. A five-year relationship ended, and I got to keep the parrot. Ah, well." He seized me suddenly, burrowed into my hair, and I hiccuped, laughing.

"Got it!" He was chewing on something happily. "One last buttercup."

"You ate it."

"Damn right. Now I am the buttercup god, and I am full of the righteous power of buttercups."

"I am full of the righteous power of scotch."

"You drank it all."

"Damn right." I balanced the cup carefully on the stones; the old crockery gleamed like pearl or the precious metal of a chalice. I stared down at it, thinking of it full, empty for refilling, complete in itself, ready to be used again, but never in that same way, since I had drunk everything there was in it. I lifted it, made a circle around it with my hands. Then I cracked it to pieces against the wall. The parrot fluttered nervously, and Michael's voice rumbled. I stared at the crockery ring still dangling from my finger. "What'd I do that for?"

He gazed down at the shards at my feet. His voice sounded hushed, as if I had done a piece of magic. "A hundred reasons. It was empty. Or it was special. Or it's too small, and you need a bigger cup. A giant cup. A King Kong cup. A cup as big as the world. What was in it?"

At the edge of the field a hundred-year-old oak, its boughs dark and tangled, was rising, glowing into the sky, as if to take the traveling moon in its wild, ancient arms. Remembering the silent years of tormented, passionate, creative chaos, I shifted close again to Michael, to human warmth. I whispered:

"Poetry."

Patricia A. McKillip was born in a leap year in Salem, Oregon, and grew up both in America and overseas. She is the author of seven books for young adults, of which *The Forgotten Beasts of Eld* won her the World Fantasy Award in 1974, and *Harpist in the Wind,* published five years later, secured her a nomination for the Hugo Award. Ms. McKillip lives in San Francisco. *Stepping from the Shadows* is her first novel for adults.